Suggs shook his head. ....d.
"I'll cover you from here."

Longarm bolted forward across the slope, digging his boot heels into the slanting, rocky turf . . . Down the slope, the *rurales* yelled and slung lead at him.

Bullets buzzed like hornets, ricocheting, shattering cactus plants, and kicking up caliche and sage and juniper branches. Suggs went to work with the Spencer, and several *rurales* dove for cover. Longarm returned fire with the Winchester, crouching and levering shells and slanting the barrel across his belly.

He turned and ran . . . across the ridge slope toward the Gatling gun nested a hundred yards farther on . . .

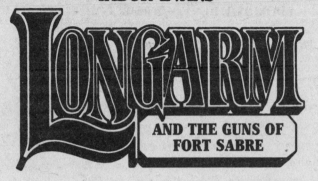

TABOR EVANS

LONGARM

AND THE GUNS OF FORT SABRE

JOVE BOOKS, NEW YORK

THE BERKLEY PUBLISHING GROUP
Published by the Penguin Group
Penguin Group (USA) Inc.
375 Hudson Street, New York, New York 10014, USA
Penguin Group (Canada), 90 Eglinton Avenue East, Suite 700, Toronto, Ontario M4P 2Y3, Canada
(a division of Pearson Penguin Canada Inc.)
Penguin Books Ltd., 80 Strand, London WC2R 0RL, England
Penguin Group Ireland, 25 St. Stephen's Green, Dublin 2, Ireland (a division of Penguin Books Ltd.)
Penguin Group (Australia), 250 Camberwell Road, Camberwell, Victoria 3124, Australia
(a division of Pearson Australia Group Pty. Ltd.)
Penguin Books India Pvt. Ltd., 11 Community Centre, Panchsheel Park, New Delhi—110 017, India
Penguin Group (NZ), 67 Apollo Drive, Rosedale, North Shore 0745, Auckland, New Zealand
(a division of Pearson New Zealand Ltd.)
Penguin Books (South Africa) (Pty.) Ltd., 24 Sturdee Avenue, Rosebank, Johannesburg 2196,
South Africa

Penguin Books Ltd., Registered Offices: 80 Strand, London WC2R 0RL, England

This is a work of fiction. Names, characters, places, and incidents either are the product of the author's imagination or are used fictitiously, and any resemblance to actual persons, living or dead, business establishments, events, or locales is entirely coincidental.

LONGARM AND THE GUNS OF FORT SABRE

A Jove Book / published by arrangement with the author

PRINTING HISTORY
Jove edition / October 2007

Copyright © 2007 by The Berkley Publishing Group.
Cover illustration by Miro Sinovcic.

ISBN: 978-0-515-14360-7

JOVE®
Jove Books are published by The Berkley Publishing Group,
a division of Penguin Group (USA) Inc.,
375 Hudson Street, New York, New York 10014.
JOVE is a registered trademark of Penguin Group (USA) Inc.
The "J" design is a trademark belonging to Penguin Group (USA) Inc.

PRINTED IN THE UNITED STATES OF AMERICA

10 9 8 7 6 5 4 3 2 1

Chapter 1

After their third waltz, Cynthia Larimer led Deputy United States Marshal Custis Long through the crowd of impeccably dressed, high-class Christmas revelers milling about General Larimer's teak-paneled, marble-floored ballroom.

A true, well-mannered thoroughbred anointed with a rare, earthy charm, Cynthia ignored no one. That, coupled with her generous spirit and devotion to the local arts, was why, whenever she was in Denver, she was the toast of the city.

She glided rather than walked through the crowd, nodding, smiling, and laughing, flashing china-white teeth as she paused for a few seconds here and there to parry compliments on her dress—a small fortune of deep-purple silk, taffeta, and velvet, with a hoop beneath the skirts, a bustle above, and a pearl-trimmed corset so tight and uplifting that Longarm had worried the poor girl was going to choke on her own tits.

A couple of handfuls of her magnificent raven hair were secured atop her head with sequined velvet, while the rest flowed strategically over her creamy shoulders. She smelled like lemons and limes with a tinge of apple blossom—an aroma so sensual that, with the girl's formfitting corset and half-exposed breasts brushing against him, Longarm had been suppressing a boner all evening.

Apparently, he wasn't the only one. Even the Governor of Colorado, Ben Eaton, took an admiring, lingering gander at the girl's wares, and Longarm thought he was going to have to punch the Interior Secretary of the United States, as the man practically groped the girl, before Longarm and Cynthia finally made it to the punch bowl.

"Oh, Custis, please tell me you're having a good time," Cynthia beseeched as he ladled up the wine-red punch in which half-lemons and apples floated and from which wafted the heady smell of cinnamon and fine brandy.

"I'm having a good time."

He handed her the filled, cut-glass cup and picked up one for himself.

"You're a terrible liar," she pouted. She nearly had to shout above the crowd of three hundred and the seven-piece brass band at the far end of the room. "But thank you for being a sport. I so wanted you to escort me to Uncle's ball!"

"Well, I've heard so much about it, I have to admit I was curious." Longarm, as he was known to friend and foe alike, glanced out over the crowd as he sipped his punch. Aside from the hired help passing silver hors d' oeuvre trays, and the band members, he was no doubt the lowest-paid fellow on the floor.

By a long shot. And waltzing with Denver's finest daughter, he'd felt like a bull in dancing slippers.

Cynthia pushed close to him and placed a hand on his forearm. "I know what you're thinking."

"What's that?"

"That you're out of place here. I want you to wipe that silly idea from your mind. Who more than the legendary Longarm—who risks life and limb every day in the pursuit of law and order on this woolly frontier—deserves to celebrate Christmas at the Larimers' annual ball?"

Longarm shook his head as he took another sip of the fruity but intoxicating punch. "That's not what I was thinking."

She stared up at him, her brown eyes glistening in the light streaming down from the crystal chandeliers. "Oh?"

"I was thinking I might have seen the face of the interior secretary's valet on a wanted dodger a while back. Bank robbery or running guns to the Injuns. Somethin' like that."

Cynthia turned her head to follow his probing eyes, her raven tresses bouncing about her shoulders. She looked back up at him, her fine lower jaw hanging. "Custis, you *wouldn't*!"

"No harm in having a private word with the gent. If I have to arrest him, though, he might start a ruckus. Hope he ain't armed." Feeling her shocked eyes on him, he waited a count, then cracked a grin.

Cynthia sucked a sharp breath and laughed huskily. "Evil man!" She set her punch cup down and grabbed Longarm's hand. "I was wrong—you *aren't* fit for civilized company." She laughed again. "Come along, Custis."

"Where we going?"

"I'm going to present you with your Christmas gift."

Longarm set his cup down and let himself be jerked along once again. "But I was just starting to have fun."

"Like a bad boy at a Mayfair party!"

They were stopped three more times, everyone wanting a word with the beguiling Miss Cynthia, the favorite niece of Denver's founding father. They slipped past the three beefy bodyguards at the ballroom door and headed up the sepulchral staircase, Cynthia climbing two steps ahead of Longarm and pulling him along with one hand while holding her skirts above her ankles with the other.

"You better not have spent much money on this old saddle tramp," Longarm groused. "That neck chain I gave you came from the mercantile on Third Street."

Cynthia turned a mock-angry look at him. "Quit fooling

3

around. We don't have much time. Uncle expects me to remain in the ballroom, charming his guests . . . all of whom bore me to tears!"

On the barrackslike mansion's second floor, they made their way through the silent, carpeted halls, Cynthia breathing heavily from the journey and the excitement of the evening. Longarm wanted to reach out and grab the girl's shoulders, pull her to him, and plant a kiss on those wide, bee-stung lips. He resisted the temptation. With the most moneyed folks in Denver milling only one floor away, it wouldn't be wise to start anything untoward. He and Cynthia had pushed their luck once too often. Just a couple of months ago, the Larimers' head butler had caught them entangled in each other's arms, naked as the day they were born, on the general's library floor!

"Oh, no, not the library again," Longarm groaned when Cynthia paused before the familiar door.

"Shhh."

She released his hand to open the ten-foot-high, solid-oak door, and poked her head into the library. "Uncle?"

She pulled her head back out. "Sometimes he brings guests up here for a private cigar, but it looks like we're alone." She grabbed Longarm's hand and pulled him inside.

The smell of old, moldering tomes and rich leather surrounded Longarm, and his heart fluttered at the remembered trauma—the butler staring down at him, one severe eyebrow arched, the inquiring voice of the general himself booming up from the floor below.

"Why the library?" Longarm groaned as Cynthia crossed the room to turn up a lamp, her own sweet aroma mixing with the library's musk, her velvet skirt swishing. "Any gift you gave me, Miss Cynthia, would mean just as much if you presented it to me in a broom closet."

"This present, my dear Custis," Cynthia cooed, curving one long, slender arm around his neck with a coquettish

4

flourish, then following it up with the other and pressing her heaving, mostly exposed breasts against his chest, "is far too precious a gift to be presented in a broom closet."

She rose up on her toes and pressed her lips to his. The kiss was like a tonic, as it always was. Her lips were like silk soaked in honey. Her tongue slid into his mouth. She cooed and sighed and mashed her breasts against him until he felt her stiffening nipples imprisoned within her corset.

He tried to push her away, but his arms wouldn't obey the signal from his brain. He was entranced by the girl, like no girl before her or, probably, after her. He wrapped his arms around her slender waist and tipped her head back on her shoulders, returning the kiss in full.

Here we go again, he thought, with a sensation of finding himself locked in a runaway stage. As he kissed her, felt her hands climb his neck to run her fingers through his hair, he glimpsed in his vision's periphery the large, night-black windows on the far side of the room, behind the general's acre-sized, leather-covered desk. The curtains were open, exposing Longarm and Cynthia to the scrutiny of the comers and goers in the yard below.

"Christ!"

Longarm jerked away from her, crossed the room, and, using the draw rope, closed the drapes over the window directly behind the desk. He turned back to the room to find her standing only inches away.

As she reached up to wrap her arms around his neck once more, he placed his hands on her shoulders and held her back. "Let's get back to the ballroom."

"Let's not."

"Cynthia, goddamnit!"

She moaned as she rubbed her breasts against his chest and nibbled his neck. "Your Christmas present, Custis . . ."

"Not getting thrown out of here and fired—my boss is here, remember?—will be present enough."

"I got you a new string tie," Cynthia said, placing his

hands on her swollen breasts. "But I thought I'd slip something in your stocking as well."

"Forget it, goddamn—!"

He stopped when she pressed both hands to his crotch. The warmth of her skin through his trousers bit him deep.

"Take it out for me, Custis," she said, lifting up on her toes to nibble his lower lip while her hands massaged his crotch.

"No."

"*Please?*"

"Under no circumstances."

"*Pretty* please?" Her nimble fingers worked his first fly button.

"This is no way for a professional lawman to behave . . . nor for a niece of General Larimer."

She giggled and poked her hand through his open fly. "With *sugar* on top?" Licking his lips and groaning, she found his iron-hard shaft, wrapped her fingers around it, and squeezed.

The floor pitched beneath his boots. "Shit."

She giggled softly, kissing him, opening and closing her hand around his shaft. "Relief is on the way, *hombre grande.*"

Suddenly, his cock sprang out of his fly like a snake leaping from its hole. The room's cool air bathed it. She laughed with delight, dropped to her knees, and nuzzled the bulging head.

He groaned and ran his hands through her hair. "You're gonna kill me yet."

She glanced up at him, smiling. "But what a way to go, eh?" She unbuckled his belt, and in a minute he was sitting back in her uncle's quilted leather swivel chair with his pants and long underwear bunched around his ankles. Downstairs, the band cut loose with a rousing rendition of "Jingle Bells," and the revelers sang along at the tops of their lungs.

Longarm tensed as Cynthia snuggled down between his knees and slowly slid her lips over his member. The hot, wet sensation and the gentle stroking of her tongue sent fireworks blossoming behind his eyelids. He let his head fall back on his shoulders as she slowly lowered her head over him, swallowing him until she gagged, then lifted her head again, lips coming free of the swollen head with a slight popping sound.

"Pretty good Christmas present, huh?"

"Not . . . bad . . ."

She licked him for a while, expertly prolonging his agony.

He'd just felt the end of his shaft sink to the bottom of her throat once more, when the door latch clicked. Cynthia froze, her lips halfway down his cock. Longarm's eyes snapped open. He stared in horror at the door, not quite believing that it was opening and that the general himself was sticking his head through the gap.

Longarm jerked, froze. There was no time to hide. He placed his hand on Cynthia's shoulder, and she scuttled farther under the desk, between Longarm's knees.

General William H. Larimer frowned. None other than the stocky, round-faced Billy Vail—*Chief Marshal* Billy Vail—stared curiously over the general's shoulder at Longarm.

"I thought I saw a light under the door," said Denver's founding father—a big, gray-headed old lion with a hefty paunch and rounded shoulders. The gold buttons on his long, claw-hammer coat glistened in the wan lamplight, as did the half-spectacles secured to his lapel with a black ribbon. He held a fat stogie in his hand. He blinked, lifted the spectacles to his deep-set blue eyes rheumy from too much punch. "Deputy Long . . . is that *you*?"

Longarm cleared his throat and placed his hand on a book that had been lying open on the desk—a thick, leather-bound tome. A quick glance showed him the author's name at the top of one page—Sir Walter Scott. Beneath the desk, Cynthia slowly removed her mouth from Longarm's cock, but she kept one hand curled around the base of it. He could feel her heartbeat in her fingers.

Longarm threw a casual, jovial tone into his voice. "Hope I wasn't intruding, General Larimer. I got a little tired from all the dancing—Miss Cynthia can really cut a rug, don't you know!—and decided to peruse your library."

Billy Vail stepped around the general, an incredulous look on his face, a punch cup in his hand. "Longarm?"

Longarm nodded at his boss. "Hi, Billy!"

"What on God's green earth are you doin' in the *library*?"

Before Longarm could reply, the general rose up on the balls of his feet, making his patent-leather half-boots squawk. "Enjoy anything you see here, Deputy. My library is open to all my guests. I'm quite the bibliophile, as you can see. You may even borrow a volume or two, if it suits your fancy—including old *Ivanhoe* there, which I was perusing before the ball."

"I might just do that."

With his own cigar, the general indicated the cherrywood box by the green-shaded gas lamp. "Help yourself to a cigar."

"You're too kind, General, but I reckon I won't be long."

"I didn't know you were a book man, Deputy."

"Neither did I," said Billy Vail.

Longarm shrugged. "I've been known to read a tome or two."

The general said, "Deputy, I've been meaning to thank you personally for escorting my lovely niece around Denver. It's a comfort to know that her safety as well as her honor is assured."

A slight snicker rose from beneath the desk, and Longarm covered it with another throat-clearing. "I enjoy taking Cynthia around town now and then. A welcome distraction from my law work, she is."

Standing beside the general, not as tall as Denver's founding father but nearly as wide, Billy Vail rolled his eyes.

"As you probably know by now, the girl's a bit head-strong, and a bit too adventurous for her own good," said General Larimer. "I'm pleased that she found an escort—a professional, respectable man, a legendary *lawman*, no less—who can keep her out of trouble."

Longarm's heart was racing like a mustang bronc out of a rodeo chute. It didn't help that Cynthia had gone back to lapping him like a dog working a pig's ear.

Longarm nodded. "It's been a privilege, General. And an adventure."

She bit him gently. He grunted softly.

"Yes, well, as I said," said the general, puffing the fat stogie, "help yourself to old *Ivanhoe* there, if it pleases you. I find Scott a romantic distraction from my daily labors."

"Much obliged, General."

General Larimer turned to Billy Vail, who stared at Longarm suspiciously, holding his glass in a hand so pudgy and soft that you never would have known he'd once been a for-midable lawdog in his own right.

"Shall we return to the ball, Marshal Vail?" said the general. "I believe this concludes your tour of my little hacienda, as I like to call it."

The general laughed and turned to the door.

Billy continued eyeing Longarm from across the room as he said, "Yes, my wife is no doubt wondering where I lit off to." He turned slowly, holding Longarm's gaze. "Enjoy the book, Custis, but don't stay up too late. Remember, you're due in my office at nine o'clock sharp."

"You know me, Boss," Longarm said, dropping his open palms on the desk as Cynthia swallowed his cock. "I'll be there, bright-eyed and bushy-tailed!"

"Yeah, I know you, Custis," Billy Vail growled as, keeping

9

his skeptical gaze on Longarm, he followed the general into the hall.

When the door latch clicked behind him, Longarm leaned back in the chair, gripping the arms, and gave a yelp as his seed exploded down Cynthia's opening and closing throat.

Chapter 2

The next morning, bright and early, Longarm hauled his tired ass up the steps of the Denver Federal Building, feeling edgy. He wasn't sure that his boss, Chief Marshal Billy Vail, knew what had been going on under the library desk the night before. But it was a good bet that he did. Billy was too good a sleuth *not* to know. Most likely, he hadn't let on because doing so would have embarrassed not only Cynthia and the general but Billy himself, given that Longarm was one of the chief marshal's senior deputies.

Longarm was probably going to get a thorough clock-cleaning or worse, and he deserved it.

A disgrace to the Denver District Court is what he was, letting a girl give him a blow job in the personal library of Denver's founding father, General William H. Larimer himself!

And not just any girl—the general's favorite niece!

If the general had discovered the lewd happenings beneath his library desk, he'd probably have found a way to get not only Longarm fired, but Billy fired as well. If, in a fit of rage, he hadn't taken a shotgun out and begun blasting, that is . . .

As for Cynthia, she'd probably be heading for some convent in Italy, never to be seen or heard from again.

Deciding he might as well get any castigation he was due over and done with, Longarm didn't exchange the usual barbs with the prissy, bespectacled lad Henry, who played the typewriter in Billy's outer office. Instead, he tossed his hat on the rack, knocked once on Billy's heavy oak door, and thrust his head inside.

He might as well go in with his chin up, on the off chance that Billy really *didn't* know. "Right on time, Chief! Bright-eyed and bushy-tailed!"

Clad in a rumpled white shirt, his sleeves rolled up his pale, hairy arms, and looking a little the worse for last night's wear, Vail peered over his large, cluttered desk at Longarm. He glanced at the banjo clock on the paneled wall. "So you are. Come on in, Custis."

Longarm sank into the red moroccan leather chair angled before Vail's desk and crossed his legs, grinning. Testing the water, he said, "Have a good time last night, Chief?"

"So-so," Vail said, shuffling through the folders stacked to his left, as though looking for one in particular. "The missus enjoyed it. She hadn't been out of the house and away from the young'uns for a coon's age. The time away did her good." The chief marshal plucked a folder from the stack and glanced at Longarm. "You have a good time?"

Longarm's heart skipped a beat. Here we go, he thought. He hiked a shoulder and flicked imaginary lint from the knee of his whipcord trousers. "Well, you know me, Chief. I can take or leave a barn dance."

"Pretty girl, though, that Miss Cynthia."

"Ain't she?"

"She's taken quite a shine to you, it seems."

Longarm grinned. "Well . . ."

"Wouldn't leave your side all night long. Danced once with the interior secretary, once with the governor, but outside of that, she was all yours."

12

"Pretty and common sense don't always go together, Chief."

Vail chuckled. "Yessir, she's taken quite a shine to you. I'd hold onto that girl if I were you, Custis. She's young and pretty as a speckled pup, and I don't even need to mention the Larimer fortune."

"I have a feelin' the general would have a little something to say about Miss Cynthia gettin' hitched to a mere lawman, Billy. You know that."

"Yes, well, he probably would, wouldn't he?" Vail smiled balefully, sighed, and donned his reading glasses. He flipped open the folder he'd plucked from the stack, opened it, and glanced at the contents.

Longarm looked at his boss skeptically from beneath his brows. If they'd come to the end of the discussion about last night, he'd have to restrain himself from leaping over Billy's desk and planting a big, wet kiss on the chief marshal's pudgy cheek. . . .

When Billy eyes stopped flicking across the top page, he flipped the folder closed. "Well, let's get down to brass tacks, shall we?" The chief marshal acquired a sour, businesslike expression as he tossed the folder across his green blotter, angling it toward Longarm, then sank back in his swivel chair, raising a hand to scratch the top of his head. "Trouble down Texas way."

Longarm gave a long, slow sigh of relief, his heart suddenly feeling like a helium balloon, as he grabbed the folder, set it on his knee, and opened it. Atop a quarter-inch-thick sheaf of typewritten and handwritten documents sat a letter written on heavy paper and bearing the seal of the War Department, Department of the Army.

"You can read the file on the train," Billy said. "The first sheet there is a simple request for you to be sent down to Fort Sabre near San Angelo for the specific purpose of investigating the whereabouts of three stolen Army Gatling guns."

13

Longarm glanced up at his boss, who sat back in his chair, fiddling with his unlit cigar. "Gatling guns?"

Billy said, "They were being transported from Fort Bliss to Fort Sabre, to help out against a band of fool Yaqui Injuns who got a wild hair up their asses to raid across the border into Texas, raising all kinds of hob with Army supply trains, stagecoaches, and ranches. They haven't done that in about two years, so it was totally unexpected.

"Anyway, one of these supply trains was attacked at night. The Army thinks it was this bronco band of Yaqui that stopped it, though none of the surviving soldiers are sure. They dynamited the train off the tracks, and stole several crates of Henry rifles and those three Gatling guns. One hell of a mess, with cars flyin' this way and that, the locomotive exploding, and barrels of kerosene catching fire. Of the twenty men assigned to the detail, only seven survived. Two of them were badly burned, but one of the other five swore he saw a swarthy gent in deerskin leggings and the calico tunic and beaded leather headbands favored by the Yaqui."

"Shit," Longarm grunted, flipping through the folder in his lap. "Three Gatling guns in the hands of those Mescin Injuns . . ." He didn't need to finish. Billy knew as well as Longarm did that the Mexican Indians were even more savage than the Apache, and as wild as or wilder than the Mescaleros and Chiricahuas had been before General Crook was sent down to southern Arizona to tame them. Some said it was easier to saddle-break a mountain lion than to civilize a Yaqui, and the Mexican government hadn't yet found a way to prove that wrong.

Billy leaned forward and placed his elbows on his desk. "Along with the Gatlings, they confiscated about twenty thousand rounds of ammo. That's a lot of ammo for an uncivilized band wreaking havoc along the border."

"Why'd they ask for me specifically, Chief?"

Longarm had no great hankering to travel to dusty, arid

west Texas. He'd been there before, and it wasn't a place you deliberately went back to—at least, not San Angelo and the grim little outpost at the edge of town. Fort Sabre was one in a string of forts situated along the southern edge of Texas and into New Mexico and Arizona to put down Indian troubles. There'd been plenty of such trouble in 1850, when Fort Sabre was built—trouble with the Kiowa, Comanche, and Apache—but most of the Indians' fire had been smothered in the last ten years.

Except that of the Yaquis apparently.

"You know damn good and well why they asked for you specifically, old son," Billy said, smiling lopsidedly. "You been down there before and you know how to handle them Injuns as well as anyone."

"You don't *handle* the Yaquis," Longarm said. "You sort of finagle your way around them, respect their fightin' savvy, and hope to get *real* lucky."

"You also know your way around south of the border."

"You're telling me I've been given reciprocity from the Mexican government to go scouting around south of the Rio Grande?"

Billy looked at him sidelong, expressionless. "No, I'm not telling you that."

"So, you're telling me that if the trail of this bronco band of Yaquis happens to cross the river into Old Mexico, I'm to hold fast and cool my heels."

Billy stuck the unlit cigar in his mouth and sucked on it. "I ain't tellin' you that neither."

Longarm gave his boss a long look, then grinned. "I get your drift. I'm not *officially* sanctioned to ride into Mexico after those Gatling guns."

"That's right." Billy plucked a lucifer from a matchbox, and scratched it to life on the green-shaded lamp. "Just like you weren't *officially* sanctioned to have your dick sucked in the general's library last night . . . but you went ahead and did it anyway."

15

"Ah, shit."

Billy's voice grew hard as he looked at Longarm through the match flame. "*Didn't* you?"

"Ah, shit!"

"*Didn't* you?"

"Come on, Chief, it wasn't my—"

"*Stop!*" Billy ordered, leaning as far over his desk as he could while sitting and poking the smoldering cigar at Longarm. "I just got one more thing to say to you, Deputy. . . ."

A soft knock sounded on the door.

Billy stared at his most senior lawdog. He said in a voice that belied the fury in his eyes, "Come in."

The door clicked, opened. Longarm turned to see a girl stick her curly, blond head in the door. Her voice was like silk.

"Hello? Marshal Vail? Am I too early?"

Billy smiled as he rose from his chair and turned toward the door. "Ah, Miss St. George, do come in!"

The girl glanced between Longarm and Billy as she sidled into the office, a small, leather grip in her hands. Longarm stared at her, befuddled at the presence of such a well-set-up little creature in the chief marshal's office, then realized that he was the only man in the office still sitting and that the girl as well as Billy were waiting for him to rise.

He jerked from his trance and rose, kicking the chair as he half-turned and gave his head a polite dip. "Ma'am, pardon my ill manners. Wasn't expecting such a high-caliber guest, I reckon."

High-caliber she was too, in her slate-gray traveling suit with a ruffled blouse that was open at the neck, exposing a deep, dark V of cleavage between short stretches of ruffled lace. She was a tall girl, about five-seven, and her straw-colored hair was naturally curly under the little feathered hat perched at a fashionable angle atop her regal head.

She flushed a little at Longarm's compliment but, like a girl used to such attention, quirked a cool, automatic smile before returning her gaze to Billy.

"Deputy U.S. Marshal Custis Long, meet Dulcey St. George."

When Miss St. George gave Longarm a nod like a queen reluctantly welcoming the garden boy into her rose patch to do a little weeding, Billy continued. "Miss St. George is the daughter of Major Artemis St. George, chief commanding officer of Fort Sabre. In correspondence separate from the official dossier, the major has informally requested that, since you're both traveling in the same direction at the same time, you escort his daughter to Fort Sabre. I understand that Miss St. George will be spending a few weeks over Christmas at the fort before returning to . . ."

"Vassar," the girl said. Turning to Longarm, she added with a patronizing air of explanation, "It's a private school for young women."

"I didn't figure it was a horse farm," Longarm said, chuckling.

"The train will be leaving at noon," Billy said, shifting his gaze to Longarm, his eyes like twin gun barrels firing volleys of silent admonitions. "Miss St. George's luggage is already at the depot, as she arrived in Denver last evening. She'll be in a Pullman car. You, Deputy Long, are to make sure that she remains safe and comfortable." He paused, put a little steel into his voice that only Longarm would recognize. "That's all."

"I'll do my best," Longarm said. If she hadn't been such a comely little lass, he'd have been none too thrilled about the chore. On long train trips, he preferred to ride in the club car, and there was nothing like having a girl along to cramp a man's drinking and gambling style.

"Miss St. George, would you please wait for just a minute in the outer office? I have one more point of business I need to discuss with Deputy Long."

"Of course."

When the girl had left, Billy came around his desk. He had such a bulldog look that Longarm found himself retreating two steps backward. Billy kept coming, his stogie in one hand. With the other, he grabbed the front of the deputy's shirt. He pursed his lips as, a good half foot shorter than Longarm, he rose up on his toes and pushed his face to within four inches of the deputy's.

"This office has a long-standing, friendly relationship with the War Department, the Department of the Army in particular, and I *will not* have that relationship compromised. Aside from making sure that girl ain't trifled with aboard the flier, you stay away from her—you hear me, Custis?"

Longarm opened his mouth to respond, but Billy jerked his shirt, cutting him off.

"If I find out that your pecker was on or in her person in any way, shape, or form, I'll be wearing it around my neck. Do I make myself clear?"

"Clear as April rain, Chief," Longarm said.

Billy grabbed the folder off his desk and thrust it against the deputy's chest. "Take this, pick up your travel docs from Henry, and get the hell out of here!"

"Wait a minute—what am I supposed to do with Miss Eastern Finishing School between now and when the train leaves."

"Show her around town. Take her to breakfast. But whatever you do—"

"Jesus H. Christ!" Longarm exclaimed, moving toward the door. "A man gets a blow job from the general's niece, and suddenly his boss thinks he's gonna demand one from every girl in town!"

He left.

Chapter 3

Dulcey St. George wasn't the best conversationalist Longarm had ever known, but he didn't hold it against her. Walking the downtown streets of Denver, populated by dusty, half-drunk stockmen and burly miners in town for supplies, she looked a little skittish.

Over a light brunch at Denver's elite Brown Hotel, he found out she'd been raised in New York and had never been west of there. Her mother had died two years ago. Since she was alone back East, both her brothers having been graduated from West Point and been stationed at western Army forts, her father had invited her to spend Christmas with him in Texas.

"He thought it would be good for my lungs!" the girl said with a nervous laugh, gesturing at her full, lightly freckled cleavage toward which Longarm dropped his gaze for only a second.

He knew when the boss was pissed, and Billy was good and pissed right now. If Longarm didn't want to be assigned to an Indian reservation up near the Canadian border next winter, he'd have to keep his distance from this little filly. Which didn't look to be all that hard. Nervous as she was, she hadn't even taken the arm he'd offered to help her across Colfax Avenue.

He had to admit, though, he wouldn't mind seeing how she looked—all naked and speckled—under that high-toned traveling suit. Not too many men would mind seeing such a long, willowy length of full-busted, sassy-hipped girl in her birthday suit.

"Well, they say the Western air is right healthful to a girl with"—Longarm's eyes dipped for another look as she picked at her coffee cake—"weak lungs."

She glanced up at him, saw where his eyes were, then frowned and hunched her shoulders.

"Deputy," she curtly, "is it too much to ask that you keep your eyes to home?"

"Pardon?"

"Away from my breasts."

Longarm looked at her sharply. He opened his mouth to tell her that he wouldn't look at them if she were displaying them like two-for-a-penny cantaloupes, but checked himself. He dropped his eyes like a chastised schoolboy and muttered an apology.

"I have to be frank here, Deputy Long." Dulcey looked up at him from beneath her beetled brows, daintily touching the cloth napkin to her full, rich lips. "I saw the way the, uh . . . girls on the street were looking at you . . . and how you were looking at them. *I* am not one of them. I am a decent girl and strictly off limits. It is your duty to see that I arrive safely at Fort Sabre, and I will hold you to that. More to the point, my father, Major Artemis St. George, will hold you to that!"

Longarm sighed. It was looking to be a long trip to San Angelo. He took the last bite of his roast beef sandwich, and gestured for the check. "We'd best start heading toward the depot."

After leaving the hotel, Longarm rented a hack and headed for his rented digs on the poor side of Cherry Creek. He

left the girl in the hack while he went into his flat to retrieve his carpetbag, which he always kept packed and
ready for quick departures. He riffled through the contents,
making sure he had enough clean underwear for what
could easily be a month's journey to the border country in
high winter, a full bottle of Maryland rye, and plenty of .44
shells.

He replaced the bottle in the bag, and tossed in a handful of the thin, dark, three-for-a-nickel cheroots from his
cigar box, then grabbed the McClellan saddle he favored,
and his Winchester rifle, and headed back to the hack,
where Miss St. George waited snootily, chin in the air, arms
crossed on her deep, freckled breasts.

They got into the Union Depot about the same time as
the flier did, so they didn't have long to wait, or much conversation to make, before they boarded. Carefully avoiding
even an accidental glance at the girl's precious tits, Longarm helped her with the two carry-on bags she'd left in a
locker, then showed her to her Pullman compartment.
Promising to check on her every couple of hours or so, then
telling her where she could find him if she needed him, he
drifted off to his assigned seat in the coach car.

The train pulled out, jerking and squawking and blowing its whistle, the coal soot floating back through the
cracked windows.

Longarm didn't see much more than brief glimpses of
the girl every few hours until late afternoon of their second
day traveling, when she appeared from her Pullman compartment to sit beside him in the coach car. She stated
primly that she was getting queasy in her cramped compartment, and thought she'd ride in the coach for a bit.

Longarm tried again to make small talk, but she preferred to stare out the window and then write a letter on
heavy ivory parchment, pooching out her lips each time
she dipped her bone-handled pen in her traveling inkwell.
Late that afternoon, after he'd read through his sheaf of

reports from Fort Sabre, he excused himself and headed to the club car for a few drinks and some poker.

He found only two men to play stud with, and though they were only playing for nickels, both folded within an hour. After they'd headed back to their wives, Longarm found himself alone in the car, with cramped legs, so he took a walk to the far end of the train, pausing for a smoke on an observation platform and to enjoy the clean, bracing December air and the snow-mantled mountains rising in the southwest.

When he got back to the club car, hoping he'd find someone else to play stud with, he found instead Miss St. George sitting at a table at the far end of the clacking car, surrounded by five swarthy, unshaven gents in sombreros and striped serapes.

Longarm had seen the five vaqueros clumped together, drinking raw whiskey and playing poker, in one of the coach cars. He'd also seen that they'd been well set up with pistols and knives. Now, it appeared, they were trying to embellish themselves with some female companionship as well.

They had the girl boxed in against the wall, two leaning toward her and grinning, one running the back of his hand through the hair falling down from her hat. She wore the look of a cornered deer, and when her eyes found Longarm standing in the open doorway at the far end of the car, she tried to get up. One of the vaqueros placed his hand on her shoulder and shoved her back down.

She gave a yelp.

At the same time, all five Mexicans turned toward Longarm. A couple smiled. A couple of others stared blankly. One fingered the big, bone-handled bowie hanging from a shoulder sheath, and flashed a silver eyetooth.

Standing behind the bar on the car's right side, the short, bald bartender shuttled his gaze back and forth between Longarm and the Mexicans with a strained, constipated look.

Longarm let the door close behind him. Hitching his cartridge belt and cross-draw .44 higher on his hips, he strolled forward, keeping his eyes on the Mexicans, who watched him closing on them with ever-increasing looks of annoyance—five dogs with a bone they didn't intend to share.

The car rocked and swayed as the wheels clattered over the rail seams. The barman remained a statue behind the bar.

Longarm arranged a friendly expression as he stopped within six feet of the table, sliding his gaze back and forth across the gang. No point in going in horns-first and possibly getting the girl greased in the bargain.

"Hola, amigos," he said. "Got room for one more?"

The one to the right of Miss St. George had one hand around the girl and the other beneath the table. He was nearly as tall as Longarm, with thick, black, curly hair falling down from his silver-trimmed sombrero. His face had been worked over with a knife a couple of times, one of the scars drawing his left eye up like an Asian's. His scraggly, tobacco-stained mustache hung down both sides of his mouth. The stench of sweat and whiskey emanated from his rumpled shirt and short, leather jacket like death from a slaughterhouse.

He curled his upper lip and squinted his eyes at Longarm. "Get da sheet outta here, brudder, or I cut your focking eyes out and feed 'em to you raw. *Comprende?*" The man's right shoulder moved, as though he were going for a sidearm beneath the table.

So much for a peaceful resolution.

Longarm's right hand shot across his waist and came up with his double-action .44.

Pow!

The bullet plowed through the Mexican's forehead, slamming his head back against the wall, which the exiting bullet had painted red with white flecks of brain and skull bone.

Miss St. George's eyes snapped wide and her mouth opened, but she didn't scream as Longarm swung his .44 to her other side. As the man to the girl's right leaped straight up, tugging a pearl-butted Smith and Wesson from a shoulder holster, Longarm's Colt belched smoke and flames, drilling a slug through the man's right temple.

His head snapped back against the wall with a sharp thud. As it began sagging slowly toward the table, the shoulders jerking, Longarm backed up and swung his .44 from right to left and back again.

The other three Mexicans stared at him through the wafting powder smoke, frozen. Two held their hands above the table, palms out. As Longarm aimed his Colt at the third man—a pudgy little hombre with a double chin and receding hairline—the man raised his hands to his shoulders and slowly straightened his fingers.

Meanwhile, the first man Longarm had shot sat straight back, head against the wall, blinking his crossed eyes as if conjuring an impossible problem. Blood ran down from the hole in his forehead, dribbled across his brow and into the inside corner of his right eye. His mouth opened and closed as he tried to speak.

As the other three watched in horror, the man's lower jaw sagged, and he slumped sideways to the floor with a thump.

The blonde stared straight ahead and down at the table, lips pursed, eyes wide, as though afraid to move.

Longarm wagged the revolver. "You boys want some of this?"

Holding their hands up, the three Mexicans slid their gazes back and forth among themselves, darting occasional looks at the two dead men before them.

"No, Señor," said the man with the receding hairline. "We mean no trouble. It was Fernando and José who wanted the gringa. Me, I doan even like Yanqui girls."

"Sí, sí!" said the man closest to Longarm, the youngest

of the group, whose mustache was like a soot smudge across his upper lip.

Longarm glanced out the window behind the men and the girl. The train had slowed to about twenty miles an hour for an upgrade.

He wagged the revolver again and stepped back. "Get up."

Keeping their hands raised, eyeing Longarm's Colt warily, the three climbed to their feet, the pudgy gent lowering his hands to push off the table, then quickly raising them again as he stood.

Longarm stepped back, gesturing toward the near end of the car. "Pronto."

They all looked at him questioningly.

"Pronto!"

They jerked to life and, kicking chairs and nearly tipping the table over, they headed for the car's rear door and outside platform.

When they stood before the door, hands raised, Longarm said, "You boys got a complicated decision to make. You can either take a bullet where your *compañeros* took theirs, or you can jump off the train."

The oldest of the three, silver-streaked hair hanging over his shoulders, tipped his head forward to regard the other two lined up beside him.

"Like I said, it's a complicated decision, so I'll give you ten seconds to make it."

"Señor," said the short, pudgy gent with the receding hairline. "We sold many cattle in Cheyenne. The check for our *patrón* is with our gear . . . in another car . . ."

"Five seconds," Longarm said, raising the cocked Colt shoulder high and angling the barrel down toward the man's head.

"Señor!" exclaimed the youngster, his tobacco-black eyes bright with trepidation. "If we do not bring the money back to—"

"Time's up!"

The little man nudged the kid with the back of his hand, then wheeled and opened the car's rear door. The others—cutting cold, angry looks at Longarm—followed him through it and onto the platform. None were wearing cold-weather gear, and they winced at the brittle wind howling off the northeastern New Mexico desert, low, sage-covered hills, and occasional sandstone rimrocks rolling past.

Longarm stepped out and pressed his back to the door. He smiled and nudged his revolver to the right and then the left. "Either side. Your choice. But make it fast. It's cold out here, and I've got a warm rye waiting for me inside."

All three glanced from right to left. Apparently deciding the north side of the train offered the best landing, though Longarm couldn't see any difference—both sides of the grade were littered with rocks and spindly desert shrubs dusted with recent snow—the pudgy gent sidled up to the platform edge.

He glanced at Longarm, then grabbed the brass hand rail. Frowning down at the ground passing in a blur, he shook his head, then kicked out with his arms and legs. He hung in the air for half a second, looking down, arms out, an anxious look on his face. As the car pulled away from him, he hit the ground on his feet and rolled down the grade, piling up against a boulder and growing smaller and smaller as the train continued up the hill.

Longarm extended the revolver at the youngest Mexican's head. The lad flinched and recoiled as Longarm said with a grim smile, "It's not too late to change your mind."

The kid turned and leaped off the other side of the platform, falling back behind the car and out of sight. When Longarm turned to the oldest of the three, he too leaped, hit the side of the track bed, and rolled, thonged sombrero whipping around his neck.

Longarm shrugged and pushed through the door. The door hadn't yet clicked closed before Miss St. George rushed toward him, threw her arms around his neck, and buried her face in his chest, her breasts heaving against his belly.

She pulled away from him, and pursed her lips angrily. "How dare you leave me alone to be ravaged by those Indians!"

She whipped her hand across his right cheek with a resounding crack. "Daddy will be *very* upset!"

Longarm's head jerked to one side and before he could stop himself, the back of his own hand smashed against her face. Miss St. George gave a scream. The slap spun her around like a top, throwing her backward, her hat and hair flying. She fell in a heap.

Chapter 4

Longarm stared down at the girl, then crouched slightly, fists balled at his sides. The bald bartender shuttled an incredulous look between Longarm and the girl sprawled on the floor in a mess of twisted skirts and petticoats, her thick blond hair hanging in disarray about her head and shoulders.

She pushed up on one arm and turned to Longarm, breasts rising and falling sharply, her passionate gaze raking across his broad-shouldered frame, down to his crotch, then back up to his face. Her red cheek showed the pale imprints of his knuckles. Suddenly, as if catching herself, the lusty look in her eyes was replaced with outrage.

"Bastard!"

"You pull a stunt like that again, you little bitch, I don't care whose daughter you are, I'll arrest you for assaulting a peace officer!"

She stared at him. Her mouth twitched, and her lips swelled. Tears filling her eyes, she sobbed like a six-year-old girl who didn't get the doll she'd wanted for Christmas. "I came looking for you because those . . . *savages* . . . were ogling me and . . . and I was afraid . . . and you weren't *here*!"

The bartender, Abe Simms, said, "Ah, Jesus, Custis, for crying out loud!"

Longarm moved toward the girl, reached for her arm. As he began pulling her gently up, he said, "When I've stowed this female where she won't be any more trouble, I'll be back to explain this mess to the conductor. Meanwhile, Abe"—he glanced at the bodies—"keep 'em warm for me!"

When Longarm had gotten the girl to her feet, he waited while she sobbed and sniffed and straightened her skirts, jerked her corset up over her cleavage, and adjusted her shirtwaist. The lawman shrugged at the incredulous barman as he led the girl toward the car's far door.

She sniffed and muttered in a voice so high and broken that Longarm could barely understand, "I thought you would protect me . . . so I followed you here . . ."

Longarm rolled his eyes and pulled her through the door. "I know, I know—and I wasn't here."

He walked her through the train's three half-filled coach cars to the Pullman, and stopped before her compartment. There were no locks on the compartment doors, so Longarm turned the brass handle, opened the door, and ushered her inside.

"But you did dispatch them fairly easily, didn't you?" Miss St. George said, turning toward him.

"Stay here and you should be safe and sound," Longarm growled, his hand still on the inside door handle. "I'll be back to check on you after—"

"Don't leave me!" she exclaimed, throwing herself against him. She wrapped her arms around his neck, pulled his head down, and closed her mouth over his, grinding her body against him.

Longarm grabbed her shoulders and pushed her away. "Jesus Christ, girl, what the *fuck* is the matter with you?"

She stared up at him. Her eyes glowed like coals, and her cheeks flushed with anger. Her hand came up in a blur and smacked his face again, even harder than the previous slap. "How dare you speak to me like that, you bastard!"

He slapped her back, but not as hard as before. He had a crazy polecat on his hands, and the only way to deal with such a beast was to let her know who was boss. Her father could jump in the nearest alkali slough, for all Longarm cared.

The slap had turned her head sideways, her hair falling across her face. She turned to glare up at him. No, it wasn't a glare. It was that lusty, almost rapturous look again. She swallowed. He turned to hightail it out of there, but before he could get full around, she leaped toward him and once again wrapped her arms around his neck and closed her mouth over his.

He tried to push her away, but she stuck to him like a predator to prey, kissing him hungrily, grinding her breasts and groin against him, jabbing her tongue between his lips. He steeled his resolve, got a firm grip on her shoulders, shoved her back, and held her two feet away. "Listen, you crazy bitch . . . !" He glanced down. One side of her corset had fallen to expose the pink nipple of her left breast. Her bosom heaved, and the nipple seemed to rise beneath his gaze.

"Kiss me, damn you," she breathed.

"No." He turned toward the door.

She placed a hand on his forearm. She didn't pull him toward her or throw herself at him. But her hand was like a hot iron through his coat sleeve, setting his whole body on fire. He lowered his gaze. Her breast had come even farther out of its binding. Oh, shit, he thought as he spun toward her, taking her shoulders again in his hands, pulling her toward him and up on the tips of her toes.

He lowered his head and closed his mouth over her parted, swollen lips, ramming his tongue between them and finding her own tongue waiting for him, wrapping around his, hot and wet and energized as if by lightning. Fury and

31

lust mixing within him, he backed her against the wall with a thud, kissing her as she groaned and rubbed the inside of her thigh against the outside of his leg. He shoved both hands inside her corset, pushing the tight garment down with his knuckles and kneading her breasts.

She groaned and sighed and tugged at his hair, thrusting her groin against his bulging fly.

There was a voice inside Longarm's head, warning him that what he was doing went against Billy Vail's direct orders, but the voice was so soft and low as to be nearly unintelligible.

He pinched the girl's hard, jutting nipples until she thrust her head back against the wall and mewed like a lust-enraged mountain lion. Finally, he pulled away from her and ripped the sleeves of her dress straight down her arms. The muslin tore with a screech. Buttons popped and flew, ricocheting off the walls and ticking across the floor.

The girl gasped, slapped him again, and called him a bastard, but there was no real venom behind it. The sting of the slap spurred him on. He lowered his head and nuzzled her firm, full breasts, white as porcelain and perfectly shaped, sucking each nipple in turn, and kneading and caressing them while she tugged at his hair almost painfully.

She grunted and shoved him brusquely back away from her, then clawed at his cartridge belt. She undid the belt with amazing agility and speed, and in a minute, the gun belt was on the floor and his pants were open. She reached down his underwear and pulled out his jutting, iron-hard shaft.

The voice in Longarm's head grew slightly louder, and it was the voice of Billy Vail: "If I find out that your pecker was on or in her person in any way, shape, or form, I'll be wearing it around my neck." Still, it was only a whisper, barely loud enough to be heard above the rumble of the iron wheels beneath the floor and the surging blood in Longarm's loins.

She ran her hand up and down his cock, the rings on her

fingers raking him until he gritted his teeth. She laughed wickedly, then mercifully stopped, knelt down, and closed her mouth over the engorged head, running her tongue around it, groaning, sighing, cursing, her lips making wet smacking sounds. When he couldn't endure anymore, he pulled her up and, with two savage thrusts, ripped the rest of her dress off, until she stood there in only her pantaloons, gasping like a landed fish.

He reached toward her low-cut, lacy chemise, but she leaped back with a breathy laugh. "I can manage the rest myself, you animal!"

That was fine with Longarm. He had his own duds to shuck out of, and he had considerable more on now than she did. He started with his boots, then ripped out of his brown tweed coat, fawn vest, shirt, twill trousers, and finally his underwear. When he'd kicked his long underwear against the door, where it caught on the handle, he turned to see her—slim, pink, lightly freckled, and naked, hair spilling down her back in gold-blond sausage curls—standing facing the compartment's outside wall. She leaned forward, hands on the bunk covered with a yellow and white quilt, her flour-white ass jutting toward him. She gave it a wag, and glanced at him over her shoulder, hair flying.

"Toddy and I always did it this way for starters"—she loosed a witchlike cackle—"because we never had the energy to do it standing up later on!"

At the moment, Longarm didn't give a rip who Toddy was. He'd already figured out that she'd been having a romping good time back East while Daddy was off fighting the Indians in west Texas.

He took her hips in both hands and slid his nodding shaft between her sweat-damp butt cheeks. Finding that her silky muff was plenty lubricated, he thrust his hips forward. As his rod slid between her slick portals, a chill ripped up and down his spine, and she lifted her head and loosed a guttural *"Uhhhh!"*

33

Longarm drove in, pulled out, then repeated the entire savage process while the girl bucked and bobbed in front of him, her head wagging and hair flying, her moans and grunts echoing off the tiny compartment's thin walls. He was nearly done when her knees and arms gave out and she sagged toward the bed. He held her up by her hips, letting her head loll atop the bunk while he continued thrusting and sliding her love nest up and down on his cock.

Finally, he threw his head back and hissed, holding her frozen against him as he let go, his seed feeling as though it were coming up from his toes to jet deep into her bowels. She blubbered and groaned as though she were being beaten with a rubber-wrapped bung starter.

When he'd emptied himself into her, he sagged down atop her back. They lay there, frozen, catching their breath for a long time as the car rocked and swayed around them, occasional blasts of the locomotive's whistle sounding a long ways away.

He pushed up on his arms, threw himself onto his back, legs hanging off the edge of the bunk. She lay so still beside him that he'd begun wondering if she were dead. He was about to place a hand on her shoulder, when she lifted her head suddenly, shoved up on her hand, and sprang toward him. She crawled over him, straddling him, her breasts swaying and nodding as she ran her hands across his chest and squeezed his upper arms.

Hoarsely, she said, "Big son of a bitch, aren't you? The thing about Toddy, he was a little man—just a little taller than me."

Longarm reached up to massage her jostling breasts while she ground against him. "Toddy's out East, is he?"

"Toddy's dead," she breathed, scuttling down to lick his hardening member. "Killed in a duel . . . for my honor."

Longarm swept her hair back from her face as she licked and nuzzled him. "A *duel*?"

"It was *very* romantic!"

Longarm had thought that even back East duels had become outdated. "I reckon not for Toddy."

She giggled, then rose up on her heels, positioning his cock beneath her, then slid down on top of it. Soon she was leaning over him, supported on her outstretched arms, and bucking against him as though on a wild mustang stallion galloping ahead of a prairie fire.

Her breasts bobbed violently four inches off the end of his nose.

When she came, she threw head back on her shoulders and screamed—fortunately, at the same time, the locomotive's wail signaled the flier's approach to Amarillo.

Longarm threw her onto her back, mounted her, and only half-seeing hog pens and horse corrals sliding past the window, finished his pleasure after one more deep thrust.

"You dirty fucking bastard!" she wailed.

Longarm had been called worse, but not at such a moment. But then, he'd never slept with anyone quite as loony as Miss St. George either, and that included a couple of Colorado mountain girls, known as "wolf women," he'd virtually been raped by in the mine shaft in which they and their crazy mountain man father had been holding Longarm captive.

Now that the haze of lust had cleared, the deputy had an undeniable urge, as strong as his hankering only moments ago, to get the hell out of the girl's Pullman compartment. He pushed off the bunk, feeling a little woozy from the tussle, and reached for his underwear hanging from the door handle.

"Don't go," the girl begged, pushing up on her elbows, her cheeks flushed, hair strands pasted to her face.

The train was slowing jerkily, and Longarm had to brace himself against the wall to keep from falling.

"I'm gonna need to fill out reports on your friends. Gettin' to be that every damn slug I sling has to be accounted for in triplicate." He shook out the underwear and stepped into it. "Faster I do, the faster the train can continue on to San Angelo."

"And the faster you can return to me, Custis?"

He glanced up at her as the train continued slowing. Custis now, was it? She stared at him, eyes aglow. His stomach fell. What the hell had he gotten himself into?

"I'll check on you again soon," he grunted.

He dressed as quickly as he could with the train jerking and nearly stopping, then starting again before halting with a lurch. He was wrapping his cartridge belt around his waist, the naked girl watching him from the bunk where she lay like a long, speckled cat, when she said, "How far to San Angelo?"

"Should be there by morning."

She smiled lustily and rubbed her bare feet together. "We'll have the whole night together."

"Ain't so sure about that, but like I said, I'll check on you again soon." Longarm pinched his hat brim at her and went out.

He'd no sooner closed the door behind him than a shoe smashed against the door's other side. The girl's voice rose shrilly. *"You bastard!"*

Longarm shook his head as he walked away, muttering, "Custis, why can't you ever just keep it in your pants?"

Chapter 5

It took so long to file his reports with the marshal of Amarillo about the club car dustup that Longarm was surprised the other three vaqueros hadn't caught up to the flier before it finally pulled away from the depot, heading south.

Reluctantly, he tapped on Miss St. George's compartment door. When she replied with a snooty, despondent "Oh, go away!" he grinned and got the hell out of there. He was happy to find that the club car had been populated with flush and eager poker players.

He checked on the girl a couple of more times that night, just cracking her door to find her safely asleep under her white and yellow quilt. After the train had pulled into the dusty, sunbaked little backwater of San Angelo the next morning, he shouldered his saddle, looped the handle of his carpetbag over his rifle barrel, and made his way toward Miss St. George's Pullman car.

As he wended through the crowd, her door opened. She stepped out in a green traveling frock cut much like the one Longarm had ripped off her delicious body the day before. She waited until the crowd had thinned in the narrow aisle, then strode toward Longarm, who'd pulled up in the open door of an empty compartment, his saddle on his left shoulder, rifle and carpetbag in his right hand.

She didn't see him until she was nearly abreast of him. When their gazes met, she turned her head abruptly away, lifting her chin higher than that of a Du Pont debutante at her coming-out ball.

"Good morning, Deputy," she said icily. "My bags are waiting for you in my compartment."

Then she pushed through the car's front door, behind a drummer in a brown derby and a checked suit, and Longarm stood glaring after her and muttering, "Back on a first-name basis, eh? Suits me."

He instructed a porter to retrieve the girl's luggage from her sleeping compartment. As he stepped out onto the station platform at the west end of San Angelo's broad main street, he felt a bee of apprehension nip the back of his neck.

If Miss St. George was angry enough about his not returning to her car last night for more slap and tickle, she might report some of the details of their wrestling match to her father, the commanding officer of Fort Sabre. Which would make Longarm's and Major St. George's working relationship a mite awkward, to say the least. Billy Vail would no doubt be informed as well, and the shit would fly!

On the other hand, Dulcey St. George was crazy, but not crazy enough to cut off her nose to spite her face. Her father no doubt figured her a virgin, the poor sap.

Or was she that crazy?

Longarm was still debating the question when he found her embracing a trim man in a blue, brass-buttoned cavalry uniform on the depot's rough wood platform. The man was only slightly taller than the girl—a middle-aged, square-shouldered, handsome figure with silver-streaked hair combed straight back from a sharp widow's peak, and a carefully trimmed, silver beard.

"Oh, Daddy!" Miss St. George said into the man's shoulder. "What a godforsaken place they've shipped you off to!" She lifted her head and looked up at him. "And it's been such a long time since you've been home!"

The major held the girl tightly, rocking her gently from side to side, his tan kepi bearing the major's insignia in one hand. "It has indeed been too long, my dear Dulcey. I'm so glad you could make it out here for Christmas." The major held her away from him and lowered his head to regard her with an anguished smile, his eyes as blue as hers. "The post is an especially lonely place this time of the year and, while I couldn't be happier that you made it, I must warn you, it is a mite on the, uh . . . rustic side."

She turned to look off down the broad main street lined with unpainted frame buildings and adobe huts blurred by the brassy winter sun and intermittent smoke puffs from cook fires. A small cattle herd was being driven through town, and the smell of fresh cow manure joined that of the town's overfilled privies and the street's ankle-deep horse shit. About halfway down the trace's right side, a couple of saddle tramps were squaring off with bowie knives, a couple of others standing around cheering.

Dulcey turned back to her father, a haunted look in her eyes. "Even more rustic than the town?"

The major laughed and hugged his daughter once more. "Why, compared to Fort Sabre, the town looks like New Orleans!"

While they exclaimed back and forth about how good it was to see each other, the porter brought the girl's luggage, and Longarm tossed the kid a silver dollar. As the porter walked away, flipping the coin in the air, Major St. George turned to Longarm standing about ten yards away, still shouldering the saddle though he'd let his carpetbag drop to the platform.

The major looked a little sheepish. "Oh, I'm sorry . . . you must be . . ."

"Daddy, this is Deputy Long," Dulcey said before Longarm could open his mouth. She gave him an inscrutable, faintly accusing look under her feathered hat as she said, emphasizing each word sharply, "*You* won't *believe* what this man has done!"

Longarm's gut tightened.

St. George, who had a weather-beaten face with a deep, jagged scar on his right temple, shuttled a curious frown from Dulcey to Longarm. Dulcey let a pregnant silence stretch, smiling smugly, before she said, "The good marshal saved me from five dirty Indians who accosted me on the train."

She looked at Longarm, her lips pursed, cheeks dimpling.

"Good Lord!" exclaimed the major, donning his hat. "That was the very sort of thing I was worried about. That's why I asked Chief Marshal Vail if you wouldn't mind escorting her."

"Oh, he watched over me quite handily," Dulcey said, looking directly at Longarm, her eyes slightly crossed, giving her a slightly demonic look.

"They were vaqueros—all newly flush and pie-eyed." Longarm stuck out his hand. "Nice to make your acquaintance, sir."

"A pleasure, Deputy Long. I've heard a lot about you."

The previous flow of conversation made Longarm eager to get down to brass tacks. "I understand you lost a few Gatling guns?"

The major turned to a young, red-haired soldier who'd been standing about twenty yards behind him, his hat under his arm. "Corporal Davis?"

The young man snapped to attention, donning his hat and rushing forward. "Yes, sir?"

"Please see my daughter and her bags back to the buggy." The major glanced at the girl's portmanteau and carpetbags.

As the corporal scampered over to retrieve the luggage from the platform, St. George favored his daughter with a fatherly smile. "Corporal Davis will drive you to the fort, my dear. I'll be along shortly, after I've introduced Deputy Long to a few of my colleagues."

The girl scrutinized the corporal, one brow haughtily arched. Longarm's balls retreated up under his cartridge belt. Pity the poor soldier. If Longarm remembered correctly from a previous trip, it wasn't a long ride to Fort Sabre. Still, the girl would most likely have the boy tied in about seven different knots by the time they arrived.

When the corporal had loaded himself down with her luggage, Miss St. George gave her father's bearded, sun-leathered face a peck, admonished him to "hurry up with that silly official nonsense" so he could begin entertaining her, gave Longarm a quick, cool glance as she turned away abruptly, and marched toward the leather-seated buggy waiting nearby in the dusty street.

The major turned to Longarm, and while the deputy might have been projecting his own feelings, he thought the man's eyes expressed a vague apprehension at his daughter's visit. "I do hope she wasn't a handful for you. Like her mother, God rest her soul, the girl can be a mite high-strung."

Longarm would have called her crazier than a tree full of owls, and as dangerous as a loaded shotgun in the hands of an imbecile, but to her father he said, "I reckon the trip wasn't long enough for me to notice."

St. George gave a relieved smile and glanced at a mud-brick, brush-roofed hovel on the right side of the main drag, which was choked with cowboys, vaqueros, and lumbering ranch wagons. A handmade shingle over the batwing doors announced RIO CONCHO TAVERN. "Several men from the fort are waiting for us over at the watering hole yonder. A humble retreat, but a favorite of my chief of scouts, and I must say I like their beer. . . ."

Longarm scooped up his carpetbag with his rifle barrel and held it over his shoulder. "We're not going out to the fort?"

"I saw no reason," said the major as he and Longarm angled into the street, quickening their paces to beat a hay cart drawn by two burros and driven by a peon in the traditional white pajamas. "I figured you'd want to head out as soon as possible to the scene of the train wreck. It's west, and the fort's east. I'll send a contingent to pick you up here in town in the morning, and you'll be on your way."

The major stopped on the narrow boardwalk fronting the tavern, through the batwing doors of which the smell of tequila and spiced pork wafted. "It is, of course, your decision, Deputy Long. You're certainly welcome at the fort."

Longarm hiked the shoulder on which his saddle rode. "I reckon there's no point, since those Gatlings weren't stolen from the fort. But I did think I'd requisition a horse from your quartermaster. Marshal Vail sees little point in depleting his office's tiny budget on a rental mount when I can get a cavalry remount for free."

The major smiled. "Chief Marshal Vail and I think alike. I've already requisitioned one of our finest bay geldings for you. Your escort contingent will lead it to town for you first thing in the morning." St. George glanced at the McClellan on Longarm's shoulder. "I should send him without leather, I take it?"

"Just a bridle and bedroll will do."

"Shall we?" The major turned and pushed through the batwings.

Longarm followed the man into the dark, smoky cantina. While the major strode into the shadows, Longarm looked around to get his bearings and to rake a quick, scrutinizing glance across the room's occupants. Having put a goodly number of men behind bars and under the sod, he never knew when he was going to walk into a tavern occupied by someone who might have a hankering to drill a slug through his head. Besides the three men at the corner table toward which the major was heading, however, there were only two other customers—peons in straw sombreros who didn't look up from their steaming bowls of *menudo* and basketed bottle of wine.

Longarm followed St. George into the room's right rear shadows, near the bar, and set his saddle, rifle, and carpetbag on a vacant table. The major, standing left of the three men slouched in rickety chairs over beer mugs and shot glasses, said, "Deputy, I'd like you to meet Captain Franklin Lewis, Sergeant Ham Keller, and . . ."

The third man at the table—a stocky, bearded gent in smoke-stained buckskins and a high-crowned, broad-brimmed hat adorned with grizzly claws and a half-moon shaped by yellow Indian beads—broke in with, "Well, look what the *cat* dragged in!"

"Shit!" Longarm exclaimed with mock exasperation. "Look what the damn cat left on the floor!"

Guffawing, the buckskin-clad gent, whose name was Lee Suggs, rose from his chair, wrapped his thick arms around Longarm's waist, and lifted the lawman two feet off the floor. "How the hell you been, you ole, badge-totin' reprobate!"

Above the man's laughter, the major said with a strained smile, "Ah, yes, you men know each other, don't you?"

"Shit, Major, me an' Longarm go back twenty years or more—long as we both been west of the Miss'ipp and dodgin' lead an' arrows an' such! Fought the Cheyenne when we were hide huntin', and Apaches when we were scoutin' for gold."

"Managed to keep our topknots when the Comanch came at us with their backs up in Palo Duro Canyon," Longarm added. He scowled with disbelief at his old friend, whom Longarm had heard was working for different divisions of the frontier Army, mostly as a scout. "How's it been that, all the years you and me been traipsin' around the frontier, we haven't seen each other in the last ten?"

"I just got lucky, I reckon!" Suggs laughed, bending straight back at the waist.

As his hat brim rose, the light from a window hit his face, revealing a milky right eye and a savage scar above and beneath it. The last time Longarm had seen Lee Suggs, he'd had no such injury. Since he and Lee had never minced words with one another, the lawman went right ahead and asked, "Lee, for chrissakes, what the hell happened to your eye? Comanches, Apaches, or Sioux?"

"A much more formidable foe than any of them, Custis!" said Suggs, grinning to show his big, tobacco-stained teeth beneath a gray-streaked, soup-strainer mustache. "My third wife!"

The old scout and buffalo hunter roared so loudly that dust fell from the rafters. When the laughter settled to a slow boil, he retook his seat, and Longarm pulled out a chair beside him and nodded to Captain Lewis and Sergeant Keller. "Nice to meet you gents. I assume that since you're here today, you'll be here tomorrow on the way to points west?"

"That's correct, Deputy Long," said Lewis, a slightly overweight man in his late twenties, early thirties, with a cinnamon beard in need of a trim and a brushy mustache. "I'll be heading the contingent, with Sergeant Keller riding second."

He had a serious air, but his rheumy brown eyes said he'd imbibed considerably more than the two beer mugs and single shot glass on the table before him. His standard-issue military tunic was missing two buttons, and his yellow neckerchief was soiled and frayed at the seams.

The unkempt uniform wasn't surprising. Fort Sabre was one of the most isolated forts in the Southwest, in some of the emptiest country outside the Mojave Desert, surrounded by the fiercest Indians on the North American continent—the Apaches, Comanches, and Yaquis—all three tribes of which had yet to be thoroughly subdued.

"Well," Longarm said when Major St. George had yelled to the barman to bring a fresh round of drinks, including a

44

couple for the Denver lawman, "I'm still sorta waiting to hear what exactly my role in this military business is. I know I was summoned because of my work against the Yaquis in the past, but hell, Suggs here has fought more red men than I have."

"Shit!" Suggs said, poking a dirt-encrusted finger through the handle of the beer glass the Mexican barman had just set before him. "No one I've ever known has fought off as many Yaquis as you did down Sonora way and lived to tell about it. And no American soldier or lawman has been that deep into that part of Mexico."

Longarm sipped his own beer, tepid but tasty after a long, nerve-wrenching ride across Colorado, New Mexico, and Texas with the major's female polecat in tow. "It might be a little late for me to put in that I had a considerable run of good luck against the Yaquis. No one fights successfully against them without it."

"Ah, you're just bein' modest, Longarm!" said Keller, laughing as he leaned back drunkenly in his chair. He wore a big, blond mustache with waxed, upturned ends on his deeply freckled face. A wing of thick, red-blond hair hung down from the tan kepi tipped back on his head. "I was in Montana at the time, and I heard all about your fightin' savvy against them savages. Besides, no American Army can . . ." He glanced across the table, deferring to the major to complete the explanation.

"Our troops can't cross the Rio Grande," said Major St. George matter-of-factly, pouring his whiskey shot into his freshly filled beer mug. "If the trail of those stolen Gatling guns leads into Mexico, which I have every reason to believe it does, we can't cross."

"I can't either—officially," Longarm said, raising a brow.

The major nodded. "But if you were to, say, get lost out there, forgetting that you'd crossed the Rio Grande, you'd be a lot less conspicuous than twenty uniformed men on cavalry remounts."

Longarm hiked a brow. "I'm to go over *alone*?"

"Nope," Lee Suggs said solemnly. "That's where I come in, Custis. But *only* me."

"Just the *two* of us?"

Major St. George looked down regretfully. "Captain Lewis and Sergeant Keller will wait for you on this side of the river. If you can make it back to the border, they'll make sure you're not pursued into Texas."

Longarm choked on his beer. "That's a relief!" When he'd gotten the beer down the right throat and had regained his composure, he said, "And how are we supposed to get the Gatling guns back to the border if we *do* happen to find them *and* find a way to wrestle them away from the Yaquis?"

"You're to secure a couple of mules and haul them back," said the major, not meeting Longarm's gaze. The man obviously knew that what he was asking was nearly impossible, but he was no doubt accustomed to giving such orders in this neck of the desert.

Longarm glanced at Suggs, who merely looked down and brushed a fly away from his beer mug. The incredulity must have been plain on his face, because St. George added, "Failing that, you're to destroy the guns. There are many mines in the area, many boom settlements. If the weapons were used against our own gold and supply trains . . . well, you can imagine how embarrassing it would be for the Army."

"I reckon it'd be pretty destructive too," Longarm said wryly. He took another sip of his beer and changed the subject slightly. "Major, how are you so certain-sure that it was Yaqui Indians that attacked the supply train?"

"It was night, and things happened rather quickly out there, but several men attested to seeing Yaquis in their customary garb."

"Yaqui look a lot like Apaches in the dark."

"Yes, but I saw them myself . . . later." The major

sipped his beer spiked with whiskey. "Two days after the incident, I myself led a contingent after the thieves. We followed a trail of twenty or more unshod horses. We were attacked three days out. They swarmed out of those rocks like hyenas, shooting repeating rifles as well as poison-tipped arrows and spears.

"I lost my entire patrol. To a man, they were wiped out."

"You were the only survivor?"

"I reckon attending chapel services every Sunday served me well. Though I was in the thick of the fighting, I was relatively unscathed except for an arrow wound in the leg. My horse was shot out from under me, and I hid in boulders. That night, I walked out, found a couple of miners who supplied me with a horse, and I rode back to the fort."

"They hit you with those Gatlings?" Longarm asked.

"No. I didn't even see the guns. They probably hadn't uncrated them, and wouldn't have known how to use them at the time if they had. They were brand-new and needed to be assembled. I'm sure that, by now, a month after the attack, they've fully assembled them and probably even learned how to use them."

Longarm had a few more questions for the major, but the conversation was soon over, the plans made, details ironed out. When St. George had thrown the last of his beer back, he turned to the captain and the sergeant, both owning the hound-dog looks of men in their cups.

The major's own voice was a tad thick as he said, "Well, gentlemen, we'd best be getting back to the fort. That gold train is due in at noon."

Neither the sergeant nor the captain looked in any hurry to leave the tavern's cool shadows, but both nodded, scraped their chairs back, and gained their feet heavily.

The major turned to Longarm, extended his hand. "Luck to you, Deputy."

Longarm nodded.

47

"And thanks once again for seeing my daughter safely to San Angelo. I'm in your debt."

"It was a pleasure, Major." Longarm glanced at Suggs, who smirked knowingly.

When the lawman had shaken hands all around, and he watched the three soldiers and his old friend, Lee Suggs, amble out of the saloon and into the dusty, sunlit street, he ordered another beer and sat frowning at it for a long time before he sipped.

Chapter 6

When the soldiers had left, Longarm sat sipping his beer and nursing a sour stomach. He wasn't sure why his stomach was sour—unless it was just the prospect of facing the Yaquis again. Facing only three of that breed was worse than confronting a herd of rampaging bull buffalo, a mine shaft teeming with sidewinders, or a Kansas cyclone.

You never wanted to face such an obstacle twice in one lifetime.

You especially didn't want to face it alone. Or with only one other man—even one as good as Lee Suggs. Two men couldn't do much against a horde of howling Yaqui snaking out of the rocks, throwing spears and loosing arrows, a few triggering Winchesters or Spencers or throwing hatchets.

Longarm figured he deserved the assignment to atone for past sins, not the least of which was accepting a blow job in General Larimer's library. But what had Suggs done?

The lawman watched the Mexican bartender, who wore a crisp white shirt with sleeve garters and a very serious expression on his clean-shaven face, set the beer and tequila on the table before him. He paid the man, sipped the fresh beer and tequila, and fired a cheroot.

Why would a band of Yaqui Indians—a mostly nomadic breed who hunted the barrancas and canyons around the Yaqui River and who mostly raised hell in their own country—have use for three 250-pound Gatling guns?

They could take out a lot of Mexican police with .45-caliber cartridges fired two hundred times per minute, but a Gatling wasn't a saddle gun. You couldn't move around quickly with it and, like the Apache, the Yaqui liked to hit and run.

They must have some specific job in mind. Another train maybe. Had they decided to try their luck on the gold caravans that the American Army escorted up from the Rio Grande? A single Gatling strategically placed could take out an entire patrol in minutes.

What did they intend to hit and when?

If Longarm could figure out the answer, he and Suggs wouldn't have to traipse all over Chihuahua and Sonora looking for them, possibly offending not only other bands of Yaqui, but the Apaches, sundry and ubiquitous gangs of border *bandidos,* and no doubt the *federales* and *rurales* as well—the Mexican police forces who didn't cotton to outsiders, including outside lawmen.

Longarm finished his beer and tequila, then stood, stretched, shouldered his gear once more, and headed off in search of the hotel that Major St. George had recommended—the only one in town that offered baths and private rooms.

After a short traipse past the bars and bordellos and milling groups of off-duty soldiers, lazing cowboys, beckoning whores, and drunken freighters, he found the hotel—a three-story wooden building that was in the process of being painted white and green by four young Mexicans. It stood in the middle of the business district and on the north side of the main drag—so new that the tang of pine still emanated from the whipsawed boards, which had most likely been cut from the high country to the east. The country around San Angelo was all greasewood thickets and bramble patches, with here and there a juniper-studded bench—barren country where jackrabbits, as the saying went, were selling shade at boomtown prices.

The hotel was run by an old freighter named Stanley who'd damaged his vocal cords shouting at so many mules over the years that he could only speak in a raspy whisper. Stanley put Longarm in room nine on the second floor, and directed him to the bathhouse out back.

The bath came with a couple of pretty Mexican girls dressed in loose skirts, low-cut Chihuahua blouses, and sandals. They heated the water, filled the tub, and even scrubbed Longarm's back, their breasts jiggling around inside their blouses like puppies in croaker sacks.

When Longarm's shaft rose up from the water as he smoked a cigar and enjoyed the girls' ministrations, the plumper of the two told him that for only two bits she'd help him relax. He didn't normally pay for "relaxation," but she was so fresh-faced, pretty, and industrious that he decided to give her free rein. If he waited until tonight to have his ashes hauled, liquor might induce him to make a bad choice of partners. He didn't want to return to Denver and Cynthia Larimer with any hard-to-kill border clap, or worse.

So he stood up and, while one of the girls shucked out of her blouse, knelt beside the tub, and took his shaft in her mouth, sucking like a young goat at a milk bottle, the other sponged his backside.

Ten minutes later, he left the bathhouse, clean and relaxed in his fresh duds and in the low-heeled cavalry boots one of the girls had spit-polished while he dressed, and headed up to his room for a nap.

It was amazing how well a man—even one who'd been sent out to tussle with Yaqui Indians the next day—could sleep after a bath and a blow job. When Longarm finally woke, Main Street was filled with long, purple shadows, and the cook fires had commenced to flavor their wood smoke with the smell of seasoned meat and frijoles.

The lawman dressed and went out for a plate of *carne asada* and a slice of apricot pie. After supper, he enjoyed beer and tequila over a poker game with a couple of off-duty enlisted men and two gandy dancers in the same cantina in which he'd met St. George, Suggs, Captain Lewis, and Sergeant Keller earlier. He decided to call it a night when his old, reliable Ingersoll read eleven o'clock and he was ahead fifteen dollars after being behind fifty-three.

San Angelo was a raucous place at night. Torches fixed to porch posts and saloon fronts showed milling, fighting men, drunken drovers and freighters staggering loudly between taverns, and two whores fighting outside a crib—half-naked, filthy, and shouting in what sounded like German.

Pistol shots rose sporadically. Horses whinnied and mules brayed. In the dark, star-shrouded plain beyond the town, coyotes howled at the rising, waning moon.

Longarm was glad to be walking down the dim, second-floor hall to his room. After a shot of his Maryland rye, he'd roll quietly, peacefully into what would probably be the last bed he'd see for weeks.

He reached for the doorknob, and froze.

The match he'd wedged between the door and the frame was gone. Which meant that either a strong wind had come up in the hall, or someone had opened his door.

Inside the room, and barely audible above the deep, slow snores rising from somewhere to his left, the snick-click of a cocking gun hammer sounded. Longarm leaped to his right as a shotgun thundered on the other side of the door, sounding like a thunderclap, blowing a pumpkin-sized hole in the door panel and showering the hall with buckshot and splinters.

On the heels of the first blast, another deafening report sounded, blowing a twin hole in the door just left of the first. By the time the wood and pellets had stopped flying around the hall, the door bore a single, gaping crater around which powder smoke wafted, filling the air with the smell of cordite.

Longarm grabbed his .44 from the cross-draw holster on his left hip, half-turned toward the door, stuck the revolver through the smoking hole, and snapped off two quick shots. The reports hadn't stopped echoing around the room, and the men inside hadn't stopped cursing, before Longarm lifted his right leg and slammed his boot flat against the door, just beside the knob.

The ruined panel flew wide, more slivers flying out from the latch. Longarm stepped inside, cocked Colt extended straight out from his shoulder. On the other side of the bed, a man in a funnel-brimmed hat crouched, his own long-barreled revolver aimed at Longarm.

The lawman ducked as the revolver roared, stabbing smoke and flames, the bullet smacking the wall behind him.

Longarm straightened and aimed his Colt. At the same time, the shooter turned and dove through an open window. Longarm's Colt barked, the bullet shattering glass as the man's boots disappeared through the window frame. There was a thud and a grunt as the man hit the hotel's porch roof below.

Longarm swung back left, cocking the Colt.

The second bushwhacker dropped his double-barreled barn-blaster as he reached for a carbine resting across the washstand. Longarm squinted down the Colt's iron sights. "Hold it, you dry-gulchin' son of a bitch!"

The man grabbed the carbine and swung it around. In the wan light from the hall, Longarm saw he was short, squat, and bearded, with a felt sombrero thonged beneath his chin. As he leveled the carbine, yelling wildly, Long-arm drilled him twice, punching him back against the wall. The carbine flew against the washstand as the man groaned, bounced off the wall, and fell on his face.

He groaned once more, twitched, and lay still.

Longarm ran to the window and looked over the sloping porch roof at the street lit by lanterns and torches. Several men and pleasure girls on the opposite boardwalk were looking toward the hotel.

Longarm followed their gazes. As he did so, a hunched shadow moved out from beneath the hotel's porch awning, hobbling on one foot toward a clump of horses tied before a saloon on the other side of the street.

Vagrant light winked off the revolver in his right hand. One of the pleasure girls on the nearby boardwalk laughed drunkenly, pointing at the man.

Longarm extended his Colt. "Hold it!"

The man raised his own revolver, squeezed off a shot. The slug plunked into the porch roof beneath Longarm, flinging slivers from a shake. Longarm returned the shot, his bullet blowing up dust a good foot shy of the bushwhacker's right boot.

The man swung around, tripping over his bad ankle, and continued hobbling toward the horses, shoving between them and reaching for a saddle horn.

The laughing whore slapped her thigh, laughing harder.

Longarm cursed, pushed away from the window, and grabbed his Winchester. Racking a shell into the chamber, he ran out the door.

Voices rose on both sides of the hall, faces peeking out through doors cracked open. The hotel owner, Stanley, stood at the top of the stairs in blue jeans and a nightshirt. One of the bathhouse girls stood behind him, holding a sheet around her brown body, eyes round with fear.

The hotel owner gestured wildly with his hands as he rasped, "What the fuck is goin' on up here?"

"Found a couple miscreants in my room," Longarm said as he pushed past the old freighter and strode down the stairs two steps at a time. "Leave the stiff where he is—I want a better look at him after I run down his friend!"

Then he ran across the lobby, threw open the door, and leaped into the street. To his left, the gimpy bushwhacker was trotting away on a dun. Longarm raised the Winchester, sighted down the barrel. "Stop or I'll blow you outta the saddle!"

The bushwhacker lowered his head and rammed his spurs into the dun's ribs. The horse lunged into a gallop. Longarm ran into the middle of the street and planted a bead on the man's back, but held the shot. There were too many people milling about the street to risk an errant round. Lowering the rifle's hammer to half-cock, he ran to the nearest clump of horses, ripped a claybank's reins from a tie rack, and leaped into the saddle.

As he backed the clay into the street, an exasperated voice rose behind him. "Hey, that's my partner's horse, you son of a bitch!"

"Deputy U.S. marshal! He's mine till I bring him back!" Longarm ground his heels into the clay's flanks.

"Thievin' bastard!" shouted the horse's owner, barely audible above the rataplan of the claybank's galloping hooves and the roar of the crowd lining both sides of the street.

Longarm kept the bushwhacker's shadow in sight as he galloped down the main drag, occasionally slowing to weave around horseback riders and wagons. Spying a group of vaqueros clustered in the middle of the street, staring after the bushwhacker, he shouted a warning. The group dispersed like spokes flying off a barreling wagon wheel.

He was out of town quickly, the night closing around him, starlight limning the greasewood and occasional piñons lining the wagon trail. The bushwhacker's shadow merged with the darkness, but Longarm could hear the beats of the horse's hooves between those of his own galloping clay.

The trail curved, dropped through an arroyo, then

climbed a low hill. Longarm pulled back on the clay's reins, and the horse skidded to a stop, snorting indignantly.

Longarm pricked his ears.

Silence except for the usual night sounds of crickets and distant coyotes. Fifty yards ahead stood a pile of wagon-sized boulders, spindly shrubs jutting from the cracks.

Beyond, the chaparral stretched flat as a pan and star-capped.

Longarm urged the claybank ahead for twenty yards, then slid out of the saddle while the horse continued trotting along the road. He swatted the mount's left hip with his rifle barrel, and the horse whinnied and broke into a gallop, heading off up trail, shaking its head angrily, reins bouncing along behind.

Longarm scampered off the trail and ran around the rocky scarp, pushing through ironwood. He continued along the backside of the boulder pile, raking his gaze along the jumbled rocks and the spindly brush, watching for the gleam of starlight off rifle bluing.

A rifle cracked.

The claybank whinnied. Hooves pounded.

At the same time, Longarm's gaze found the silhouetted figure wedged between two boulders at the scarp's right shoulder. The man was facing the trail. Smoke wafted in the still air around him.

Longarm's right boot clipped a stone.

The figure atop the scarp swung around, and the rifle flashed and roared. The slug burned a line across Long-arm's right cheek, spanging off a rock behind him.

Longarm snapped the Winchester to his shoulder and levered three quick rounds. The bushwhacker jerked, froze, swayed backward. Then his arms spread, the rifle clattered to the rocks, and the man fell forward.

Longarm stepped to the side as the body rolled to the bottom of the scarp and into the willows. It came to rest on its back.

Longarm stood over the body. The man had thin, sandy hair and a gray-streaked beard. No distinguishing marks except a dime-sized mole on the nub of his chin. A green bandanna was knotted around his neck, and the open eyes stared up at Longarm, glistening in the starlight. The blood oozing from his chest and belly added a copper tinge to the smell of creosote.

Longarm prodded the man's shoulder with his boot toe. "Who are you, you son of a bitch?"

Chapter 7

It took Longarm a good forty-five minutes to track down both the dead bushwhacker's horse and the claybank, to load the bushwhacker onto his dun, and to haul him back to town.

The sheriff was waiting for Longarm outside the hotel with a peeved look in his eye and whiskey on his breath. Longarm suspected the local lawman was more chafed at having his evening interrupted than at a deputy U.S. marshal having been ambushed in his town. From the pistol fire Longarm had heard earlier, and continued hearing sporadically, the two men Longarm had killed would be part of a much larger pile before the sun rose in the morning.

Even with better lighting, Longarm recognized neither of the two dead bushwhackers. The hotel owner didn't know them, the sheriff didn't know them, and neither did the two deputies who showed up later, also with liquor on their breath, one with lipstick on his unshaven cheek.

"Somebody's gotta know 'em," Longarm said, flicking cigar ash on the body of the first man he'd killed as he, the hotel owner, and the three lawmen stood over the two dead men sprawled on the hotel's front porch. "They didn't just fall outta the sky."

"Well, shit, I seen 'em around *the saloons*," said the shorter of the two deputies—a bandy-legged little gent named Hutton. His breath smelled like a beer vat. "I just don't know their *names*. I figured they was just freighters waitin' on another freightin' job."

"Well, ask around," Longarm said. "If there's anything that galls my ass worse than getting bushwhacked, it's not knowin' *who's* bushwhackin' me and *why*!"

"I understand you're sore, Deputy Long," said the sheriff, whose name was H. J. Burkette, though he never said what the initials stood for. "But I'll be giving the orders around here, if you don't mind. My deputies ain't *your* deputies, since you're *federal* and I'm *local* and you never even had the good form to let me know you were in *town*!"

Longarm took a long, exasperated drag from his cheroot. It was he, Longarm, who'd been bushwhacked in the sheriff's town, and Longarm wasn't obligated to pay the man a professional visit since Longarm was here on *federal*, not *local*, business. He opened his mouth to give the sheriff an earful, but held himself back. The inebriated lawman and his drunken deputies obviously didn't have the sense of trash-heap rats. An argument would only further delay a good night's sleep.

Biting his tongue, Longarm apologized, politely asked the sheriff to let him know if the dead men's identities became known, then headed upstairs to bed down in a room without a cow-sized hole in its door.

He was up at first cockcrow. Many people had tried to kill him over the years, either to avoid capture or to exact revenge for dead or incarcerated friends or family.

These two bushwhackers might not have fit into either slot, but might have tried to kill him for some other reason entirely. He'd have slept a lot better if he knew what that reason was . . . and whether more bushwhackers were looking to turn him out with a shovel.

He washed, shaved, packed his carpetbag, and was just finishing up a breakfast of fried lamb with potatoes and eggs when he saw a short column of soldiers, riding two abreast, pull up in front of his hotel on the other side of the street. Captain Lewis, Lee Suggs, and Sergeant Keller rode at the column's head.

Longarm paid for his breakfast, shouldered his gear, and headed outside. The air was cool, morning-fresh and flavored with breakfast fires. The dawn was a salmon wash hovering low in the east.

"Here, Captain," Longarm called as a corporal mounted the hotel's front porch.

The corporal stopped as the rest of the column turned toward Longarm. Suggs grinned and hailed him. Captain Lewis smiled through his unkempt beard. "Ah, an early riser." He glanced at the private riding directly behind him and leading a leggy bay. "Your horse, Deputy Long. The best in our stables."

Longarm only grunted. The bay might have been the best in the stables, but it was a typical Army remount—sickle-hocked and too long in the leg and narrow in the cannon for long, hard desert travel. He should have rented a half-broke, desert-bred mustang from a local livery.

Sucking a cheroot, Longarm laid his McClellan across the bay's back. Buckling the straps and attaching his saddle boot, he looked over at the nine young soldiers flanking the major and Sergeant Keller. They looked like schoolkids to Longarm—Johnny Raws freshly graduated from Jefferson Barracks. Except for the corporal, who appeared to be in his early twenties, none looked over sixteen. All were blond and fair-featured—northern European immigrants, no doubt, who'd decided to try the Army instead of milking cows or driving freight wagons. The sunburned faces looked both weary and harried.

61

Reading Longarm's mind, Sergeant Keller chuckled. The pitch of the chuckle told Longarm the man had already taken a couple of pulls from a bottle. "Not to worry, Deputy Long. These boys don't look it, but they're veteran Injun fighters. I handpicked 'em myself."

"Good to know," Longarm said, grabbing the reins and swinging into the saddle.

A moment later, Captain Lewis called out, a little louder than necessary at this early hour, "Forwaard . . . *hooo*!"

At a slow trot, the detachment headed west along the main street. A couple of dogs ran out from an alley to bark and nip at the bays' hocks. The sergeant roared angrily, and both dogs turned on dimes and retreated back to the alley from which they'd surfaced.

Lee Suggs gigged his horse up beside Longarm, who rode slightly behind the captain. "I know what you're thinkin', Custis, but these boys really are the best we have. We've been hit hard by desertion, as Fort Sabre's a little too hot and dry for these kids—not to mention the Injun and owlhoot trouble of late."

"I'll take your word for it," Longarm said, hipping around to glance back at the young men trotting behind him, most pimple-faced and sullen and looking none too happy about heading out after Yaquis. "But if we're going to ride toward Old Mexico with young'uns, I wish we had a few *more* of 'em."

"I hear that," Suggs said. "But chances are you and me'll be heading into Mexico alone anyways, while these boys dog-paddle around in the Rio Bravo."

The column wound its way through the low brown hills northwest of San Angelo. At midday, they arrived at the scene of the train wreck—a twisted, charred jumble of cars lying to and fro amidst large heaps of scraped dirt and uprooted shrubs. Dried blood stained the battered metal. The dead and wounded had been carted off, and the tracks had been repaired, the new rails stretching in a quicksilver line to the far horizon. While the deep tracks of the Army ambulances remained, any sign the attackers had left had been covered by wind and rain.

As the soldiers built a couple of coffee fires from crushed sage branches, Longarm smoked a cheroot and looked around, finding little of importance—only a couple of charred saddlebags, some Army hats and spurs, part of a rifle. He kicked aside a half-burned coach seat, and was ambling toward the overturned caboose when a guttural sound rose behind him.

Clawing his .44 from his holster, he wheeled, raised the revolver chest-high, and thumbed back the hammer. A coyote peeked out from around a detached, bullet-dented vestibule. The animal was showing its teeth around what remained of the desiccated, sand- and blood-crusted hand in its mouth. The ring on the hand's middle finger winked in the sunlight.

The scavenger stared at Longarm for a couple of seconds, raising its hackles, then turned and loped off through the brush. Longarm depressed the Colt's hammer and lowered the gun to his side.

A laugh sounded. "I see you haven't lost a step on your draw anyways!"

Longarm turned. Lee Suggs sat his star-faced dun, leaning forward on the saddle horn, his buckskin tunic dark with sweat. His lean, bearded, sunburned face was shaded by his broad-brimmed sombrero. A greasy red bandanna fluttered around his neck. He'd been burned and jerked by the desert so long that he could have passed for a mestizo, a half-breed Mexican Indian.

"I thought the soldiers carted off all the bodies."

Suggs hiked a shoulder. "The hand must've been buried in the wreck. That brush wolf found himself a treat."

Longarm holstered his six-shooter and looked around, squinting against the light. The winter air was mild, but the brassy sun was intense. "You find anything?"

"Nothing that would put your mind to rest."

Longarm arched a brow.

Suggs said, "We ain't been together in a month of Sundays, Custis, but I can still tell when somethin's stuck in your craw. You ain't convinced it was Yaqui that attacked the train, are you?"

"No, I reckon I'm not. But don't ask me why. It's just a feelin'."

"You don't think they're sophisticated enough to blow a train off a track—that it?"

"It's not their style, Lee. The Yaquis travel in small groups, and they like to travel light. To take down a train and steal its cargo, they must've had twenty, thirty warriors out here—a long way from their stomping ground. Not only that, but how did they know they were hitting a supply train? Must've done some reconnaissance or—"

Suggs stared darkly at Longarm, but he curled his lip in a smile. "Or had somebody working the inside."

"There you go."

"Well, shit," Suggs said, pulling a tobacco braid from his tunic pocket, blowing something off the end. "I hope you're right. I'd rather dance out here with anyone but those fucking Yaquis. Hell, they'll cut off a feller's eyelids so's he can watch 'em use his balls for pincushions." He extended the tobacco braid toward Longarm. "Chaw?"

"No, thanks."

Longarm tramped back to where the soldiers, including Lewis and Keller, were gathered around the coffee fires.

Longarm, Suggs, and the soldiers pushed hard the rest of the day. They stopped an hour before good dark, their breath and their horses' breath puffing in the chill evening air, and the captain posted four stationary pickets on low ridges fifty or a hundred yards out from the bivouac.

Around a low, snapping fire upon which a coffeepot chugged languidly, Longarm, Lewis, Keller, and Suggs played a desultory game of poker while sipping coffee laced with whiskey. When the officers rolled up in their blankets, Longarm and Suggs spent another forty-five minutes catching up and chuckling over past adventures. Suggs yawned, relieved himself behind a greasewood shrub, bade his friend good night, and turned in. The young soldiers murmured quietly in their own bedrolls, while the officers snored deeply under their low-canted kepis. Suggs's own snores quickly joined the choir.

Longarm had one more pull from his rye bottle, entertaining visions of Cynthia Larimer in nothing but the maid's apron she wore one night a couple weeks ago, in the Larimers' kitchen, bent forward over the table. Then, chuckling, he tipped his hat over his eyes, and willed himself to sleep.

They were on the trail again at first light, after a hurried breakfast of hardtack, jerky, and coffee. The farther they rode southwest toward the Rio Grande, the more the desert expanded around them, the faultless blue sky rising, the sparse growth becoming even thinner. The mesas, scarred by deep gullies, grew taller, redder, and broader. A couple of tabletop buttes were so large that it took over an hour to get around them.

The country was so vast and imposing, in fact, that Lewis called in his outriders. Longarm suspected the captain was afraid they'd get lost. Even Longarm, who'd tramped around southwest Texas several times before, was in awe of the country's beguiling, deadly breadth.

It seemed all the more deadly when they came upon the site of the ambush St. George's men had fallen victim to. A detail had been sent out to bury the bodies, and the nineteen graves, mounded with sand and rocks on the bank of a boulder-choked arroyo, were covered with buzzards. A couple bodies had been dug up and dragged off by a mountain lion, judging by the tracks.

Several winter rains had fallen since the attack, blotting

out most of the sign left by the attackers. Cartridge casings littered the area, most belonging to common rifle makes and calibers. There were spears and arrows as well—all with Yaqui markings.

Suggs held up a spear with a blood-crusted tip hammered from scrap iron, a red feather braided Yaqui-fashion just above.

Longarm scowled with chagrin. "I found a sombrero with the same marks."

"That's because it's those damn Yaquis done this, Custis. It's time to face facts."

"Goddamnit," Longarm grumbled as he swung back into his bay's saddle. "I always did hate when you were right, Lee."

Suggs chuckled and ran a sleeve across his mouth, streaking more tobacco juice in his beard than he removed.

The old scout managed to spy a couple of unshod hoof-prints pointed south. When the column rode out after a brief pause to pay their respects to the fallen soliders, the old tracker rode scout, returning to the column once every hour to report on what, if anything, lay ahead. His third time back, he halted the dun ahead of Captain Lewis and threw an arm out, indicating west.

"Nothing much, but I spotted black smoke rising just over that low ridge yonder, Captain. Want I should check it out?"

Longarm turned to scrutinize the western horizon. A thin streak of smoke, so thin as to be nearly invisible, rose from behind a low, red camelback.

"Could just be a prospector's fire," Lewis said, "but I reckon you'd better check it out. Private Walters! Private Floyd! Accompany Mr. Suggs!"

"I'll tag along," Longarm said.

He and the two privates detached from the column, and followed Suggs through the gentle swells of caliche-covered desert. They rode for a good fifteen minutes, rifles laid across their thighs, before they pulled up in a mesquite thicket between two knolls.

"Quiet now, boys," Suggs instructed the soldiers. "Yaquis have a third ear."

Longarm and Suggs stole up the face of the knoll, the soldiers following with their trapdoor Springfields held at port. Like Suggs, Longarm stopped near the knoll's crest, removed his hat, and peered over the lip.

A hundred yards away, blurred figures flitted about the chaparral carpeting a slope rising toward the base of a sandstone wall. Animal-like whoops and wails rose faintly on the still, afternoon air.

A rifle cracked, the shot echoing off the sandstone wall.

Suggs glanced at Longarm. The scout's eyes were wistful. "We could send for the column . . ."

"It might be a trap. Best to scout it first." Longarm levered a fresh shell into his Winchester's breech, off-cocked the hammer. "I'll head up that ravine toward the ridge. Why don't you and one of the soldiers take the arroyo?"

Suggs nodded and turned to the soldiers kneeling behind him and Longarm, their eyes wide. "Floyd, you come with me. Walters, stay here. If you see a mirror flash, hightail it back for the column, hear?"

"You got it," Private Walters said, giving Private Floyd a subtle smirk. His gaze grew thoughtful. "B-but what if you don't come back and there ain't no mirror flash?"

Longarm and Suggs shared a glance. "Send the column home," they both said at the same time.

They moved out.

Chapter 8

Hearing several more rifle reports, agonized screams, and jubilant whoops, Longarm cat-footed around the knoll's shoulder and into the ravine. It took him fifteen minutes to make the base of the sandstone wall, where the ravine dead-ended in a pile of spindly brush and boulders. No doubt an underground stream gushed out of the wall in the spring or in wet years.

An especially anguished wail rose as Longarm climbed out of the ravine and, holding the Winchester in one hand, crawled through the loose gravel along the wall's base. He bit his cheek as he crawled. He'd heard the sounds of Yaqui torture before; there was no doubt that that was what he was hearing now.

He crawled up the side of a gravelly crease. Four feet from the crest, he doffed his hat and edged a look over the top, through a couple of dead sage shrubs.

On the crest of the next crease over, a man lay spread-eagled on his back, wrists and ankles tied to stakes. He wasn't wearing any clothes—at least, none that Longarm could see beneath the thick coat of dark-red blood. Black-haired and bearded, the man turned his head from side to side, large gut rising and falling heavily.

Just beyond him and right lay a dead mule with a saddle. Beyond the mule, three brown-skinned figures in deerskins and straw sombreros darted around in the brush, howling and dancing, one holding a bloody scalp high above his head and whooping shrilly.

Longarm donned his hat, stood, and ran over the crest of the crease, up the next grade, and hunkered down beside the bloody man—a Mexican—still shaking his head and breathing heavily. Blood sprayed from the man's lips with every labored breath. His eyes had been gouged out, nose hacked away, privates cut off. By the way he was yowling, his tongue had probably been ripped out as well.

Wincing against the tortured man's screams, Longarm looked up the rise. The three Yaquis were dancing and whooping, but facing in the opposite direction from Longarm.

Keeping an eye peeled on the celebrating Indians, Longarm slipped his knife from his right boot well, scuttled up beside the half-dead man's right shoulder. He set the knife's point against the tender skin beneath his right ear. With a quick, jerking motion, he swept the razor-sharp blade across the man's neck, in an arc ending under his other ear.

Longarm removed the knife as blood spurted out from the severed carotid artery, gushing across the man's chest. Almost instantly, the man's screams stopped.

Up the grade, one of the dancing Yaqui froze and wheeled toward Longarm, a startled look on his round, savage face. Longarm whipped up his rifle, thumbed the hammer back.

"Dance about this, you fuckin' savage." The rifle bellowed and punched a slug through the Indian's throat. The brave whipped back, twisting sideways and shrieking as blood sprayed from the hole in his neck.

The other two Yaqui wheeled toward Longarm, their dark faces like shocked masks above the stunted chaparral.

70

As Longarm rammed a fresh shell in his Winchester's breech, both Indians loosed a howl and leaped toward him. Longarm drew a bead on one who was snaking a Spencer carbine, hanging from a leather lanyard, around toward his chest. The shot took the man through the head, stopping him instantly and throwing his head straight back on his shoulders.

As Longarm levered the Winchester, the other brave burst through the brush, sprinting toward him with a knife in one hand, a cap-and-ball revolver in the other. The man whooped and yammered as he ran down the grade, leaping stones.

Gunfire rose in the distance behind him, and several Yaquis shouted in their guttural tongue.

Longarm fired at the zigzagging figure, the man's long, black hair whipping from side to side, craggy teeth bared. The shot plunked into the ground behind him, blowing up gravel. The man's black eyes glistened as his enraged gaze locked with Longarm's, and he shrieked like a sow in an abattoir.

Still on his knees, Longarm cursed as he rammed another round into the chamber. The brave was twenty feet away and closing fast, crouching and zigzagging, moccasins grinding gravel.

Longarm aimed, allowing for another dodge, and fired. The slug sliced through the slack in the man's calico shirt, and pinged off a rock.

The Indian howled, stopped, aimed his revolver at Longarm's head. The lawman ducked as the gun's hammer clicked against the firing pin. The brave stared down at his revolver, shocked.

"Your hammer dropped on a dud, old son." Longarm gained his feet slowly, grinning. "Go ahead—give it another try."

The Indian snapped his eyes back to Longarm. Gritting his teeth, he thumbed back the hammer and snapped up the revolver. Before he could pull the trigger, Longarm crouched and drilled him twice through the chest.

As the Indian staggered backward, dying, there was a whooshing sound. Something nipped the back of Longarm's neck. A clatter rose to his right, and he turned to see a wooden arrow skidding along the sand and gravel, careening toward the base of the ridge.

Footsteps thudded on his left.

He whipped around too late to bring his Winchester up. Another Yaqui was running up the crease, a bow in his left hand, a quiver bouncing around on his back. He lowered his head and bulled into Longarm with a wolflike howl.

The stocky warrior threw Longarm onto his back, the rifle flying off to the side. Longarm clutched the man's wrist and, rolling off his shoulder, flung the man over his head.

"Ay-eeeeee!" the warrior shrieked, turning a somersault and landing on his back with a thump.

In less than a second, he bounded back to his feet, a cedar-handled bowie knife in his hand.

On his left shoulder, Longarm reached across his belly, grabbed his Colt, and fired.

Pop!

The Indian grunted as the bullet plunked through his belly, punching him two steps straight back. He glared at Longarm and had just started gritting his teeth, when a fist-sized hole opened in the man's forehead, spewing blood and white matter onto the ground near Longarm. The rifle report echoed off the sandstone wall and flitted off across the basin. At the same time, the Yaqui's head snapped down, chin smacking his chest. He staggered forward as though drunk, grunting, sighing, and farting, then dropped to his knees and curled up like a baby put down for its nap.

Longarm looked up, expecting to see Lee Suggs standing up the slight rise toward the sandstone wall. The lawman frowned, incredulous. Not Suggs, but a beautiful, dark-skinned woman in a deerskin skirt and knee-high leggings leaped down from a boulder near the base of the ridge. She sauntered toward Longarm with a smoking carbine in her hands, long, chestnut hair winging out from her chiseled, olive-colored face as she turned her head from side to side, raking her gaze around cautiously, her brown eyes cool.

She stopped and turned to Longarm, who lay staring up at her, still not sure he could believe his eyes. Maybe the brave had killed him and he was in heaven. The girl's heavily accented voice brought him down to earth.

"Who are you, gringo?"

Longarm looked around. The shooting had tapered off but his nerves were still on alert. "Deputy U.S. marshal." He turned back to the girl. "Who're you?"

She nodded at the dead man whom Longarm had put out of his misery with his bowie knife, and a vaguely hateful look came into her eyes. "I worked for him." For a second, he thought she was going to spit in distaste for the man.

Longarm stood and picked up his rifle, still raking his gaze around the brush and clusters of rocks and boulders—anywhere a Yaqui might be holing up, waiting for him to turn his back. "Doing what?"

Before she could answer, Lee Suggs called from the brush sixty yards west. "Custis, you all right?"

Longarm turned to where Suggs stood, nearly hidden by the chaparral, waving his battered Stetson in one hand above his head. Longarm waved back, indicating he was all right.

Suggs said, "Any more dirty Yaqui snakes still kickin' over there?"

"Not sure," Longarm yelled. He turned to ask the girl if she knew how many Yaquis were in the raiding party, but she was jogging into the brush behind him, her skirt buffeting across her russet thighs, thick hair bouncing on her bare shoulders.

"Hey, where you goin'?" She disappeared into the heavy chaparral, and Longarm frowned. For a second he wondered if she'd been with the Yaqui. But she wouldn't have shot one of her own.

He kicked around the brush, inspecting several gullies lying perpendicular to the ridge wall. He found no more Yaquis, but he stumbled across two dead mules that had probably belonged to the dead Mexican, ambushed when he'd been watering the mules at a spring. Both mules now tainted the spring with several slick rivers of liver-colored blood. The packsaddles were stuffed with dry goods and mining supplies, but nothing had apparently been touched. Though the braves whom Longarm had encountered hadn't been painted for war, they'd obviously been more in the mood for killing and torturing than stealing.

Longarm plucked several cigars from a burlap pouch spilling canned goods and boxes of matches. Lighting a cigar, he looked around for the girl. No sign of her.

Later, he found Suggs standing on the knoll where he'd seen him before. The scout stood atop a low boulder, holding a small, round mirror high above his head, signaling Private Floyd with sun flashes. Nearby, young Private Walters crouched over one of the four Yaquis lying dead in the area, inspecting the brave's beaded boot moccasins.

"All clear over there," Longarm said to Suggs. "How 'bout over here?" He added doubtfully, "Any Gatling guns?" The braves who'd attacked the Mexican prospector were most likely a small passel of younkers out sharpening their horns to while away the winter. Getting into a young Yaqui princess's doeskin bloomers was a lot easier if you could show off your warrior's prowess with a scalp or two.

"No such luck." Suggs stared out over the chaparral to the ridge upon which Private Floyd was a blue silhouette ringed with yellow by his Army-issue neckerchief. "Me and Walters brought down four, but three got away. Slipped around us. We scared the shit out of 'em, I reckon.

Weren't expectin' us and the dumb younkers didn't post pickets."

Chuckling, Suggs lowered the looking glass and jumped down from the boulder. "They're headin' straight for that pass yonder, looks like."

Longarm looked at a notch between two distant, plum-colored stretches of mountain—the Jacarita Range, if he remembered correctly. "Headin' back to the main camp, no doubt."

"And probably the Gatling guns."

Private Walters interrupted. "Hey, Mr. Suggs, think I can take these here Injun moccasins? They fit me like they was sewed on my foot!"

Longarm and Suggs turned to the young soldier, who'd kicked off his left boot and was donning the moccasin, walking around to test the fit.

"You know regulations, Ephraim," Suggs said. "But shit, I won't tell on ye."

Longarm only vaguely heard Suggs's response. Looking around, he'd spied the girl sitting atop a nearby knoll, a pair of saddlebags lying at her feet, a canteen hanging from a braided leather cord around her neck.

He walked over. She didn't look at him until he'd been standing before her for several seconds. Apparently, she'd hid the gear in the brush when she'd been scrambling away from the Yaquis, who would have had quite a time with such a beauty if they'd found her.

Longarm grinned, his eyes bright with roguish irony. "Come here often?"

Her face was implacable, wisps of hair blowing around her high, chiseled cheekbones. She wore nothing under the deerskin vest, the two lapels of which were tied together by whang strings wrapped around small, silver discs. There was a two-inch gap between the lapels, exposing her deep, dark cleavage.

She wasn't in the mood for nonsense. "You have horses?"

"Sure."

"Which way you go?"

Longarm pointed toward the distant, blue range jutting against the southern horizon.

"I go that way too."

Footsteps grew behind Longarm. He turned to see Lee Suggs and Private Walters walking toward him. The private had hung the moccasins from his cartridge belt.

Suggs shifted his glance between Longarm and the girl, and a wry look came into his eyes. "Leave it to you, Custis, to find a pretty girl out here in the middle of nowhere."

Chapter 9

On the way back to the knoll upon which Private Floyd waited, Longarm told Suggs as much as he knew about the girl—that she'd been with the prospector when he was attacked by the Yaqui, that apparently she hadn't fancied being with him all that much, and that she wanted to go back to Mexico.

"All we need's a female tagging along," Suggs grumbled, glancing over his shoulder at the girl walking well behind Private Walters, a disinterested expression on her regal face. "She's liable to slow us to a damn crawl."

"I wouldn't talk too loud," Longarm said. "She knows how to use a rifle."

"What the hell we gonna do with her?"

"Maybe we'll find a campesino out here, slip him a few dollars to see that she gets to where she wants to go."

Suggs cast another glance over his shoulder. "Not bad-lookin', is she?"

Longarm cracked a smile as he stared straight ahead. "I hadn't noticed."

They gained the ridge where Private Floyd was waiting, smoking a cigarette, the young soldier's eyes flicking instantly to the beautiful señorita. Suggs waved a hand in front of the private's starry eyes, then ordered him to return to the column as fast as his horse would carry him.

"Tell Lewis that me and Longarm are going to follow the three Yaquis in hopes they'll lead us to the Gatlings. After you boys have buried the Mexican prospector here, track us to the Rio Grande, set up camp, and wait for us. Private Walters will ride that far, in case there's anything we need him to report to Lewis. Clear?"

Floyd said he understood.

"Take the girl with you, Private. She's Lewis's prob—"

"No!" The girl stalked up from the mound she'd been sitting upon, holding her carbine, barrel down, in her right hand. She stepped between Longarm and Suggs and stared angrily into the old scout's craggy face. "I want to go to *Méjico!*"

Suggs glanced at Longarm, then returned his eyes to the girl. "That just ain't gonna happen, Señorita. At least, not now. Me and Custis got official business south of the border, and we can't have no—"

"I am sure you both have *superior* tracking skills, but the Yaqui know how to cover their trail. They do not leave as much trace as a rattlesnake." Her round, molasses-colored eyes shifted between Longarm and Suggs, settled on Longarm. "I will take you to the Yaqui encampment."

Longarm frowned skeptically.

"I recognize the markings." The girl glanced at the beaded moccasins hanging from Private Walters's cartridge belt. "They are from the Black Widow Mountain band of Yaquis—a *muy* poisonous band that has been attacking gold camps and blowing up railroad tracks in Méjico. I know where they go when they are not raiding. I can lead you."

Suggs glanced at Longarm again, then with a dry chuckle returned his gaze to the girl. "How would you know where those Yaqui are holed up?"

"I was raised in the Black Widow Mountains. I have seen their encampment."

Suggs slid a glance to Longarm. "You know the place, Custis?"

Longarm scowled as he stared at the girl. "Heard of it. Never been there." To the girl, he said, slitting one eye, "Not to sound ungrateful, but why would you help a couple gringos?"

The girl's eyes hardened. "Two weeks ago, a group from their band kidnapped my sister from Sandoval's shack. I wish to get her back." She raised her rifle, lifted her chin defiantly. "Maybe paint my face with a little Yaqui blood as well."

Longarm hooked his thumbs in his cartridge belt. "Out of the question, miss. The Black Widow Mountains are a good fifty miles from here. And we don't have any spare horses."

She looked around. "The horses of the Yaqui you killed . . . ."

Suggs shook his head. "The three that got away took the whole remuda." He glanced sidelong at Longarm. "Them havin' those extry horses is gonna make 'em extry hard to catch up to, old son. And like the señorita says, a Yaqui don't leave much fer footprints."

Longarm studied the old scout. "What're you sayin'?"

"That we're corn-holed if we do, corn-holed if we don't."

"Don't what? Take her *along*?"

Suggs nudged the lawman's arm. Longarm followed him to the edge of the knoll, facing south into the misty blue distances beyond the Rio Grande.

"We could take Walters's or Floyd's mount." Suggs glanced back at the girl staring after him and Longarm haughtily, holding her carbine across her breasts. "They could double up as far as the Rio Grande. And shit, she *does* look tough enough to wrestle a grizzly bear. I might be kickin' myself in twelve hours, but she don't seem the type that's gonna complain about the lack of feather pillows and lilac water."

Longarm looked at her. Her doeskin skirt buffeted around tan, well-muscled thighs—the legs of a girl who'd spent time on a horse. He had to agree that she could no doubt hold her own on a long march across the desert. While he knew where the Black Widow Mountains were located and had talked with prospectors from the area, he had no idea where the Black Widow band of Yaqui might be holed up. Finding the Indians would be like looking for a single raindrop in a snowmelt stream.

Having a Mexican civilian guide Longarm and Suggs wasn't regulation, but then neither was sending a cavalry scout and a U.S. marshal south of the Rio Grande.

"Let's shake a leg," Longarm said, and headed for his horse.

Privates Floyd and Walters trotted off toward Lewis and the cavalry column, looking none too happy about riding double. Longarm, Suggs, and the girl, whose name Longarm learned was Raquella Concepción, mounted up and lit out in the direction the three Yaqui had fled.

The Indians had left clear tracks for several miles, but then they'd spread out and zigzagged across the bare surface rock between sheer cliffs, making them tougher to follow. At good dark, Longarm, Suggs, and the girl bivouacked in a dry arroyo a mile south of the Rio Grande. They risked no fire, eating jerky and hardtack washed down with water.

Longarm and Suggs passed a bottle back and forth a couple of times. Longarm offered the girl a drink. In reply, she snootily rose from the rock she'd been sitting on.

"Go ahead, drink yourselves crazy. *Hombres blancos borrachos locos!* Just remember I sleep with a knife across my belly."

She stomped off a good twenty yards from the men, and curled up in her blankets, resting her head against her saddle. Longarm and Suggs shared a curious glance.

Longarm and the scout were up before dawn. They rolled their blankets and leathered their horses while the girl continued sleeping several yards away, between a slope and a Joshua tree.

Suggs led all three horses off to a spring, and Longarm remained behind with the girl. Sitting on a rock near the low coffee fire they'd allowed themselves, Longarm was about to roust Raquella when she stirred suddenly. He couldn't see much of her in the heavy dawn shadows, but her brown outline rose up out of the blankets and stretched. She gave a tired groan, then, wrapping the blankets around her sleek, high-busted form, tramped barefoot over to the fire.

She sat down across from Longarm, pushing up close to the warm flames, and he poured her a cup of coffee. Handing the steaming cup to her, he said, "Sleep well?"

She only grunted. Her hair was mussed about her face. The blanket was pulled taut across her heavy breasts, outlining each one clearly. She stared into the flames as she lifted the tin cup to her mouth.

"There's jerky in them saddlebags beside you," Longarm said, holding his coffee cup with one hand, smoking a cheroot with the other.

She glanced at him, frowning thoughtfully between wings of rumpled, chestnut hair. Then she looked at the saddlebags. She opened the flap and pulled out a hunk of jerky. She bit off a chunk.

Chewing, she said, "I am sorry for my rudeness . . . last night about the drink. Sandoval was a drunk. He did depraved things when he drank the pulque."

"How'd you come to be with Sandoval?"

"He purchased my sister and me from my uncle when my aunt died. For two mules and a rifle."

"Where're your parents."

"Dead. My father was a yanqui prospector from Arizona. My mother was Apache. We wandered Sonora and

81

Chihuahua looking for gold and silver, until a sickness took them both." She sipped the coffee, staring over the rim into the fire. "My sister, Rosa, she is frail. If she still lives, I must find her . . . find a good home for her." She looked up suddenly at Longarm. "Maybe you marry her? You seem good man. You need a wife?"

Longarm opened his mouth to speak, but Raquella jumped in with: "When I say frail, I mean only she is small. But she is tough. A good worker. She is *muy bonita* . . . and young . . . only sixteen."

Longarm was glad to hear hooves clomp nearby. He turned to see Lee Suggs's shadow leading the three horses up from the spring. "Ain't exactly in the market for a wife," he said, rising and tossing his coffee dregs on the fire. "But I'll let you know if I change my mind."

They made good time throughout the morning, traversing a wide valley with several different mountain ranges rising in three directions around them. Red tabletop mesas and rocky buttes humped closer by. The sun vaulted over the cobalt sky, shunting shadows around.

In the summer, the heat would have been like a furnace. But in December, the sun was a warm relief from the night's penetrating chill.

They didn't stop for lunch, but only to water and rest the horses every two hours. In the saddle, trotting and walking their mounts by turns, they nibbled jerky, hardtack, and canned peaches.

About three in the afternoon, Suggs rode up alongside Longarm. "You see 'em?"

"Yep," Longarm said.

He glanced to his right. Two men in steeple-crowned sombreros traversed a low hill in the far distance, about three or four hundred yards away—little more than specks between two massive ridges.

Longarm had seen three men a short time ago. Earlier, he'd spied four watching them from a granite-faced ridge, apparently not caring that their spyglass winked in the sunlight, giving them away.

Longarm turned to Raquella riding to his left. *"Bandidos?"*

"Or *rurales*," she said, staring straight over her horse's bobbing head. "They are one and the same out here."

There wasn't much doubt about what their shadowers might be after—the horses, the girl, a rousing diversion, or all three.

After the three outriders had disappeared down the backside of the distant hill, Longarm and Suggs saw no sign of them again that day.

As the sun fell, casting giant, bone-chilling shadows down from the ridges, they made camp in a narrow canyon, near the mouth of a tunnel some prospector had carved into the side of the mountain, searching for a gold or silver lode most likely.

There was a small, stone house whose roof had long since collapsed. Fronting the house lay a well surrounded by a crumbling stone wall. A good four or five feet of water stood at the bottom, and Longarm, winching a bucket up, discovered that it tasted sweet.

"Good water," Suggs agreed, sipping from his tin cup. "It'd make a mighty good stew . . . if we had something to put in it besides desiccated corn and old jerky."

Longarm was cleaning his bay's left rear hoof with a pick. "When I scouted up the canyon, I spied a couple of grouse. Wouldn't want to give our camp away with a rifle round. You still good with a slingshot?"

The scout finished off his water, knelt down, and produced a slingshot, made of ash and cow gut, from his saddlebags. He glanced at Longarm with a look of mock injury. "Custis, I'm offended you had to ask me that question."

When Suggs had walked up the narrow canyon, Longarm built a fire in a niche in the canyon wall, under a rock overhang, where it couldn't be seen easily from any direction.

Then he spread his blanket roll and laid down his saddle. He hadn't seen the girl since she'd finished gathering firewood and headed into the brush down the canyon with a canteen and a sliver of soap from her saddlebags. No point in worrying about her until she'd been gone another ten or fifteen minutes or so. She didn't look the sort to linger over a bath, but she was a female after all.

He got a pot of coffee started and set his Maryland rye next to the dented tin cup that had seen its share of campfires over the years, then headed into the brush to take care of nature. Since the girl was around, he ventured off a good thirty yards through the brush, stopped, and opened his fly.

He'd been waiting to piss for a while, so he tilted his head back and let it go. As the stream cascaded into the brush, he cast his glance along the rim of the far ridge, vaguely looking around for interlopers. When he finished, he shook a couple of times, then tucked himself back into his pants, crouching and bouncing a little, making the required adjustments.

He turned to his left, and froze. The girl stood before him, her back to the ridge. She wore a bemused smile as she clutched a sweater to her breasts with one hand while holding the sliver of soap in the other. Her canteen and a sponge rested on a nearby rock.

Her long hair was damp, and it hung down her tan, bare shoulders. Strands of it clung to the rounded globes of her breasts peeking out around the blanket.

Longarm's face was hot, but his loins felt as though they'd been touched with an electrified wire. He cleared his throat. "Sorry. I didn't see you there."

She dropped her gaze slowly down his chest and belly to his crotch, then lifted it quickly back to his eyes, her own cheeks flushing with embarrassment. "I apologize, Señor Long. I was going to say something . . . but then . . . I didn't." She hiked a shoulder and dropped her gaze to the ground.

Longarm wanted to reach out and grab her. Nasty business, though, getting involved with a girl on the trail. Too distracting. Against his will, he said, "I reckon I'll let you get back to your bath," then started back toward the fire.

Later, Suggs returned to the camp in the twilight, holding up a dead turkey and grinning like a schoolboy who'd plugged his first gopher. It was a tough old tom, but with wild herbs that Raquella foraged from bays in the canyon wall, it made a delectable, hearty stew. All three ate hungrily and, after they'd enjoyed a last cup of coffee spiked with rye—even Raquella—Suggs took one more straight shot, then picked up his Spencer and wandered off to keep the first watch.

Longarm rolled up in his blankets near the fire. As it was a cold, high-altitude night, Raquella spread her own roll near the crackling flames, which they'd left high enough to provide heat, but not so high as to attract visitors.

He didn't know how much time had passed after he'd laid his head back on the saddle and tipped his hat down over his eyes, but he heard the soft crunch of gravel under a bare foot. He smelled the girl close by, and poked his hat back from his forehead. In the fire's wan glow, Raquella was a curvaceous shadow above him, blocking out the stars.

"Do not get the wrong idea," she whispered. "It is cold, and I wish only to share your warmth."

She dropped to her knees, then rolled up against him, drawing her heavy, ragged quilt up to her chin. She slid her face against his shoulder, pressed her breasts against his ribs—two warm mounds swelling out beneath her blanket.

"Buenas noches," she said.

Longarm winced as he tipped his hat over his eyes. "Right."

Chapter 10

It didn't take Raquella long to fall asleep. In only a minute or two, Longarm heard her slow, measured breaths as she breathed into his shoulder, her breasts pressed into his ribs.

She groaned softly and curled her right leg over his left.

The warmth radiated from the girl's delectable body, tickling the lawman's primal urges, preventing him from drifting off. It kept him lying there grimacing as he squeezed his eyes closed, trying to conjure cold but restful images—a cabin in the mountain snow by moonlight, a train stretched across a dark Dakota plain. Images that would distract him from the picture in his head of those firm, perfect breasts stamped against his side . . .

That would distract him from the sensual warmth of her thigh crossed over his, and from the erotic sighs and groans that periodically escaped her half-open mouth.

Finally, he poked his hat off his forehead, tossed off his blanket, and sat up. She gave a startled whimper, and her eyes fluttered. She grunted as she scuttled over to the blanket he'd vacated, tugging her own tattered quilt over her shoulders, and snuggled down against his saddle.

In seconds, she was breathing deeply again through

those slightly parted lips he had to hold himself back from kissing.

He cursed, stood, shook out his boots to dislodge possible black widows, then stomped into them quietly and wrapped his gun belt around his waist. When he'd pulled on his sheepskin coat and gloves, he grabbed his rifle and headed out toward the well coping, a pale smudge in the darkness, fronting the dilapidated stone house.

A rifle lever rasped to his left. He turned to see the bulky figure of Lee Suggs moving toward him at a crouch, breath puffing against the stars.

"It's me, Lee. Go on back to the fire. I'll take over the watch."

Lowering the Spencer, Suggs walked toward him. His blanket coat was rife with the smell of countless mesquite fires. "What's the matter—can't sleep?"

"Nah."

"Don't tell me you've gone jumpy."

"Yeah, I reckon those damn *bandidos* just turned me all to jelly. Might as well stay up and let you get your beauty sleep, hoss. Lord knows you need it."

Suggs chuckled quietly and strolled toward the fire glowing dimly through the brush. "If you get scared, give a whistle and I'll come hold your hand."

"Much oliged." Longarm stared off down the canyon as he took his rifle under his arm and raised the sheepskin's collar to his jaws. It was as cold as the Panhandle out here.

He took a couple of scouts up and down the canyon. Hearing and seeing nothing, he found a chute up the far ridge, climbed it, and looked around on the rock-scaled crest. Only stars and sage, with occasional gnarled clumps of greasewood and catclaw growing out of the cracks in the stone.

He sat on a low, flat-topped boulder and peered over the canyon—a narrow gash of oily darkness framed by crenellated, starlit ridges. No sounds except occasional sighs of a vagrant breeze sending the chill down the back of Longarm's collar. The oily smell of the creosote made him yearn for a cigar. But a *bandido* lurking behind a rock or shrub clump could spy the glow, even shielded by a cupped palm, a good two hundred yards away.

From behind him came the muffled sound of rock striking rock. He whipped around, thumbing the Winchester's hammer back. He stared into the darkness, able only to penetrate a few feet.

About thirty yards straight out, there was a flinty scrape, as if someone were clambering around on rocks. Slowly, holding the Winchester out from his chest with both hands, he moved forward. The hair on the back of his neck pricked. Someone could be crabbing around behind him, drawing a bead on him.

He stopped suddenly. A black stretch of narrow cleft stretched before him, like a black, jagged-edged carpet laid across the caprock. Impossible to tell how deep it was, much less if someone were down there.

Longarm squatted five feet back from the edge and, laying his rifle across his thighs, pricked his ears, listening, squinting his eyes to pick out anything moving amidst the soupy darkness.

Silence.

A sudden, feline snarl rose sharply. Longarm's heart leaped and his rifle snapped to his shoulder. Two bright dots glowed against the cleft's far wall, about ten feet down from the top and inside the silhouette of a bobcat's head, ears standing like triangles. Longarm held fire. No point shooting the beast, and loosing a shot that could be heard clear to the border, if he didn't have to.

The cat's eyes lifted and the snarl sounded again, lifting the hair under Longarm's collar. At the same time, a shadow slid across the brush to his right. Longarm whipped around. A huge, man-shaped figure loomed before him, capped with a steeple-crowned sombrero. Starlight glinted off steel.

Throwing his shoulders forward, Longarm leaped straight back, toward the cleft behind him. The Mexican grunted as the blade sliced the air about three inches shy of Longarm's belly.

Longarm leaped forward, snapped his rifle up, and slammed the stock against the *bandido*'s right cheekbone. The man cursed loudly in Spanish as he twisted around and fell in a heap. Longarm took another step forward, and was about to level the Winchester when his attacker, fast for his size, bounded off his heels and drove his head into Longarm's belly.

Longarm flew straight back, the ground coming up to smack him hard. The blow ripped the Winchester out of his hands. It bounced off the Mexican's right shoulder and hit the ground with a thud. The Mexican landed on Longarm's chest, rose to his knees, swung his arm back, and brought a savage fist across the lawman's left cheek.

Longarm's head reeled. Fireballs exploded behind his eyelids. As the Mexican cocked his fist again, fiercely grunting, spittle flying from his lips, Longarm forced up his own left arm, parrying the man's punch. The blow felt like a two-by-four slammed against Longarm's forearm. Pain lanced up and down the limb and into his hand and shoulder.

Longarm rammed his right first across the man's jaw. From that angle and distance, it wasn't much of a blow, but it threw his attacker off balance, giving Longarm the advantage for about one second. He used it to kick up with both legs, grunting and cursing with the effort, throwing the man sideways.

Longarm rolled away. The man reached for the silver-plated revolver on his hip, slipped it out of his holster with a rasp of steel against leather.

Longarm lunged forward, kicked the gun out of the man's fist. It popped, flinging flames skyward. Then the big Mexican was on his feet again, crouched forward, sidestepping. Longarm faced him, fists bunched, breathing hard.

The Mexican grinned savagely, teeth flashing in the vagrant light. He bolted toward Longarm, feigned a left jab, then swung a haymaker up from his ankles. Longarm ducked.

The fist whistled over his head. The Mexican yowled with rage, his spurs chinging off gravel.

Longarm lunged forward, slung his fist against the man's right ear so hard his knuckles felt as though they'd rammed a barn wall. Blood oozed like glistening oil in the darkness, and Longarm's fist came away wet. The blow didn't faze the man. He jerked his head up and buried his right fist in Longarm's gut.

The air left the lawman's lungs with a loud *"Ugghhh!"* As Longarm bent forward, knees buckling, gasping, he caught a glimpse of two copper-colored eyes glinting in the darkness at the lip of the ridge.

The cat.

Before Longarm, the Mexican bent down, came up with the lawman's rifle. Longarm tried to draw his Colt from the cross-draw holster, but he couldn't pull his arms away from his gut.

"Oh-ho, gringo!" the Mexican whooped. "Your time is up, eh?" He raised the rifle to his shoulder, squinted down the barrel at Longarm kneeling before him. "When you get to hell, say hello to—"

The cat screamed.

The big Mexican tensed as a gray-brown shadow leaped out of the darkness, melding with the big man's silhouette. There was a flash as the rifle exploded, the slug plunking up dust near Longarm's left boot. The Mexican lost his grip on the long gun and screamed as the big cat drove him to the ground, the cat snarling so loudly that the din seemed to echo off the stars and sear into Longarm's bones.

"Gringo, help me!" the Mexican cried. *"Shoot!"*

The cat buried its head in the man's neck. The tail lashed like a whip. The man's legs thrashed, fists flailing against the gray-brown hide. He wailed, voice rising to a shrill crackle. The cat whipped him from side to side, trying to break his neck. Wet, sinewy chewing and sucking sounds rose as the powerful jaws and razor teeth ripped fresh meat.

Beneath the din, Longarm vaguely became aware of gunfire rattling from the direction of the main canyon. Suggs and the girl had been ambushed. He had to get down there.

Eyeing the grisly wrestling match before him, he managed to force a breath down his tight chest. He grabbed his Colt from the cross-draw holster and thumbed back the hammer, then heaved himself to his feet. Holding one arm across his belly, he sidestepped the cat and the dying Mexican, tracing a wide circle around the duo as he looked around for his rifle.

It lay about fifteen feet away, the barrel extended over the gorge's lip. Keeping his pistol trained on the cat and continuing to hear the cracks of angry gunfire emanating from the ravine in which he, Suggs, and Raquella had bivouacked, Longarm scooped up the Winchester. The Mexican fell suddenly silent in mid-shriek. His body flopped from side to side as the cat, holding its right front paw on the man's blood-soaked chest, continued ripping out the man's throat as though trying to pull a knot from a tree stump.

Backing away from the jostling shadows, the smell of blood and viscera mixing with the fetid, wild smell of the cat, Longarm holstered his six-shooter and took his rifle in both hands.

"*Bon appétit*, kitty," he said in a pinched voice, still able to take only shallow breaths as he turned and stumbled back toward the main canyon and the rataplan of angry gunfire.

He was halfway back to the ridge crest when he managed to suck back the pain in his throbbing cheek and head and lift his heels in a stumbling sort of run. At the lip of the ridge, breathing hard, he looked into the canyon and about fifty yards to the right. In the tar-pit darkness, guns flashed like fireflies, the reports sounding a half second after each flash. Bullets barked off stone, the echoes squealing off the canyon walls.

By the flashes, there appeared to be four or five shooters fronting the bivouac, from which two sets of shots could be seen—one regularly, the other intermittently. Apparently, the girl was helping Suggs hold off the *bandidos*. They couldn't hold them off long, however, before one or two of the *bandidos* ran around their flank.

Longarm hustled back to the trough by which he'd climbed the ridge, and scrambled down. Twice, his boots slipped in the loose rock and he fell. The second time, he rolled three times before slamming his rifle butt down and breaking the fall.

When he reached the canyon bottom, he stumbled along the ridge base, heading toward the first set of gunshots, about twenty yards out from the ridge. As he traced a meandering course through the boulders and shrub clumps, the first shooter's shots grew louder. Longarm moved around a boulder and stopped. The man's outline, complete with steeple-crowned sombrero and silver spurs, took shape behind another boulder just right of a spindly piñon. Longarm leaned forward over the rock, the rifle resting on the rock before him.

The *bandido*'s carbine leaped, spewing flames from the barrel. As he lifted the gun to jack another shell in the chamber, Longarm extended his Winchester. *"Amigo!"*

The man turned his head, jerked with a start. White teeth flashed in the dark oval of his face. The Spencer repeater swung toward Longarm, who pumped three shots into the man before he could level his carbine. The man, bent backward against the boulder, was still gurgling and grunting as Longarm sprinted past him and stopped.

93

Fifteen feet away, a silhouette in a short jacket and low-crowned sombrero stood between a boulder and piñon tree. He held a rifle straight up and down before him.

As Longarm jacked a fresh shell in the Winchester's breech, the silhouette jerked, snapping the rifle down. The barrel stabbed smoke and flames, the slug sailing to Longarm's left and, with a dull smack, drilling the head of the *bandido* draped across the boulder.

Longarm dropped to one knee, levered two shells into the silhouette. The man groaned, knees bending. Longarm didn't wait for him to drop.

He sprang off his haunches, ran down the canyon twenty more yards, and stopped near a low mound of up-thrust shale and gravel.

Only a couple of widely spaced shots sounded off to his left. A horse whinnied. The raucous rattle of spurs and muffled Spanish voices grew faint.

Suggs's voice lifted, clear in the sudden silence. "Custis, you out there?"

"Here, Lee."

At the base of the far ridge, boots thudded and spurs chinged. Suggs's breathless voice quivered as he ran down the canyon. "We better get the rest of those bean-eaters, or there'll be more!"

Thumbing fresh shells into his Winchester's loading gate, Longarm jogged forward, toward the din down the canyon, where the *bandidos* were apparently retreating to their horses. Suggs was right. They had to assume there were more *bandidos* where these came from; border bandits usually ran in packs of fifteen or more. If Longarm and Suggs didn't eliminate the rest of this group, the survivors would doubtless summon more, and there would be hell to pay by sunrise.

His Winchester heavy with fresh brass, Longarm ran through the brush and boulders, leaping and bobbing and ducking under pine branches. A rifle boomed to his left, echoing. Return fire pattered ahead, a rifle flashing.

On the other side of the canyon, Suggs cursed.

Longarm stopped. "Lee?"

"Caught a graze!" Suggs yelled hoarsely. "Get those sonso'bitches!"

Longarm ducked under a mesquite tree, brushed passed a boulder, and stopped. Three shadows bobbed and weaved in the darkness before him—three horseback riders heading for the canyon mouth, hooves clattering, leather squawking, trace chains rattling.

Longarm raised the Winchester to his shoulder, quickly aimed, and fired. A man screamed and lurched forward. His horse whinnied shrilly and jerked sharply to one side.

Longarm ejected the spent shell, aimed at the shadows of the two other fleeing *bandidos*, and pumped six shots in five seconds, the rifle leaping in his hands, the smell of hot iron and powder smoke peppering his nose.

Amidst the barrage, men cursed and screamed. Horses whinnied. Hooves scuffed and clanged off rock.

Longarm ran forward along the wild horse trail cleaving the canyon, a pale, thin line in the night. He stopped suddenly, pricked his ears to listen. One of the Mexicans was wailing, but it was too dark for Longarm to see him or any of the others he'd hit.

All at once, the wail grew into a shrill, clipped scream. A thud, as though a body collapsed in the brush.

Longarm frowned. Holding the rifle straight out from his right hip, he moved forward.

He stopped again, squinted into the darkness. A slender shadow grew on the trail before him. He raised his rifle. The shadow stopped.

A girl's voice: "Señor Long?"

Longarm lowered the rifle. "Raquella?"

The shadow continued growing on the trail, mocassined feet crunching gravel, thudding softly in the powdery dust. She stopped six feet away, clad in only a brown wool poncho

95

and moccasins. Her legs were bare. She looked up at Long-arm as she wiped the blade of the long stiletto in her right hand with the yellow bandanna in her left. Her eyes glistened in the starlight.

"They are finished."

She threw away the bandanna and brushed passed him, striding toward the camp.

Chapter 11

After making sure their staked horses had come through the attack unharmed, Longarm and Suggs dragged off all six of the dead *bandidos,* excluding the one the mountain lion was still probably dining on, to a brush-choked gully. The *bandidos'* mounts had all scattered out beyond the canyon's mouth, which wasn't good because other *bandidos* might find them and backtrack them to the canyon, but nothing could be done about that tonight.

"You think they were after the horses?" Suggs asked when they'd tossed the last body into the gully. His bandanna, with which he'd wrapped his bullet-burned upper arm, formed a red line on his buckskin sleeve.

"The horses, the girl," Longarm said, testing his bruised lower jaw as they started back toward the camp. "Probably both . . . and anything they might find in our saddlebags."

"I just hope they weren't part of a bigger group that's gonna get lonesome and come looking for 'em."

"By the time they do, we'll be long outta here."

"What happened to your jaw?"

Longarm chuffed. "They were expecting a lookout, sent up a big bastard to turn me inside out. Damn near did too."

"Stop his clock?"

"Fed him to a mountain lion." They were approaching the fire, which the girl had built up and next to which she sat cross-legged, sharpening her knife on a whetstone. Longarm glanced at Suggs. "How's your arm?"

"I'll keep spattering whiskey on it. It'll be all right." Suggs chuckled, stopped, and turned to Longarm. "Shit, Custis, ain't we gettin' too old for this dog play?"

"I was about to ask you the same damn thing."

As Longarm turned to continue to the fire, Suggs grabbed his arm. The old scout was about two inches shorter than Longarm, and he looked up at the lawman with an insinuating half smile as he said softly, "Say, what was she doin' layin' against your saddle earlier, all curled up in your blankets? You and her . . . ?" He made a lewd gesture with his hands.

Longarm dropped his jaw with mock indignation. "She was cold, Lee!"

"Hell, I'm a warm body. She didn't crawl under *my* blankets!"

Longarm walked over to the fire, squatted to pour himself a cup of coffee. "You all right?" he asked Raquella, who continued to sharpen the stiletto—long, rhythmic strokes.

"*Bandidos* are nothing," she said without looking up. "Now, the Yaqui . . ." She smiled coldly, the blade making snick-snick sounds on the stone. "Of them, I am afraid."

Longarm rose, stared grimly into his coffee cup, and repeated an old adage he'd heard on his last trip to Mexico. "Only fools are unafraid of Mojave green rattlers, black widows, and Yaqui Indians."

Only the girl slept for the remainder of the night. Longarm and Suggs, energized by the *bandidos'* attack, sat on the ground, backs against the well coping, sipping coffee and chatting about everything from old times to the Black Widow Mountains to the price of whores in New Orleans.

When the night began to lift from the canyon and birds started singing, mud swallows quarreling along the canyon walls, they rose and brushed themselves off. While Suggs stepped away to take a piss, Longarm walked over to where the girl slept in his and her blankets near the fire.

He stared down at her, admiring her beauty as she slept on her side, blankets pulled up to her chin, knees drawn up to her belly. Her hair fanned out across his saddle, her eyes lightly closed, the dark lashes slightly upturned at the ends. Her jaw was a long, straight line, and her neck was smooth as polished cherrywood. He wanted to lean down and nuzzle her awake. Instead, he put a hand on her shoulder.

Her eyes opened instantly and she turned her head to stare up at him, startled.

"Time to go," he said gently.

She sat up and raised her hands above her head, stretching, and the blankets fell away from the poncho she wore over her vest. The poncho was oversized, and it billowed out to reveal her cleavage. Her voice was faintly accusing. "I was cold."

He kicked dust onto the fire's gray ashes. "We need to get on the trail in about ten minutes. No time for breakfast, I'm afraid."

She stood and strode off into the brush. She stopped suddenly and turned back to Longarm, shaking her hair back from her face. She put her chin down and furled her brows skeptically. "You have no woman at home?"

Longarm didn't so much consider Cynthia Larimer his woman as a partner in sin. "Nope."

The girl's eyes held his, and the corners of her lips rose in a coquettish smile. Then she turned sharply and strode off through the brush, the blankets parting to reveal the backs of her taut, brown thighs.

Longarm watched her fade into the brush, felt his long underwear grow tight. "Damn." He loosed a long sigh, then headed off to retrieve the horses.

He was leading the mounts back to the bivouac when he stopped suddenly. Suggs stood before the well coping, staring down canyon with his rifle in his hands, chin up, back straight. Gray light was beginning to filter into the canyon, and a light breeze brushed the creosote and sage and rushed against the ridgetops. Longarm followed the scout's gaze, but he couldn't see anything from his position.

"What is it?"

Suggs spoke softly. "Riders. Headin' this way."

Longarm continued leading the horses forward until he stood off Suggs's left shoulder. He stared down the trail, beginning to hear the soft thud of horse hooves moving lazily toward them.

"Bandidos?"

"I don't think so. A second ago, I spied *rurale* gray and a silver badge."

Longarm squinted down the trail meandering through boulders and chaparral, turned a wry glance to Suggs. "Damn, your eyes are good."

"How do you think I keep my topknot out here?"

"If these are *rurales*, I hope you're as good at talking as you are at seeing."

Suggs spat and looked around. Longarm knew he was wondering if they should make a run for it. "Forget it," Longarm said quietly as the first rider pulled around a boulder and rode straight toward him and Suggs. "Our horses ain't saddled and Raquella's off tending to nature. And we best not get *too* hasty about shootin' *rurales*."

The rider wore a gray uniform tunic, gray slacks with red stripes, and a leather-billed officer's hat adorned with the silver eagle insignia of the Mexican rural police force.

His head swung around from left to right. Glancing straight ahead, his dark eyes widened suddenly. He drew back on the reins of his gray mare, and unsnapped the cover over his revolver as he barked orders in Spanish.

The line of riders behind him broke from the trail and

came up on both sides of him, four galloping through the brush and rocks to his right, three swinging wide of the well coping on his left, and halting ten feet before Longarm and Suggs. Dust rose in the dim gray light. Hooves thudded, leather squawked, and horses blew.

The crowlike *rurales* sat before Longarm and Suggs, in their dove-gray uniforms with gilt edging on the sleeves, their dirty gray sombreros bearing silver eagle insignias on the crowns. They aimed their Springfield trapdoor carbines over their horses' heads, stocks snugged to their cheeks.

The lieutenant rode up between two young *rurale* privates sitting dusty duns. He turned his horse slightly, and aimed his Colt Navy .44 straight across the gray's right shoulder, jerking the barrel for emphasis as he loosed a short string of nearly incomprehensible Spanish. His gaunt, hawkish face was red beneath his natural brown, and his flint eyes spat fire.

Holding his hands chest high, palms out, securing the reins of the three horses under his right thumb, Longarm glanced at Suggs. "I think he wants us to drop our gun belts."

The lieutenant shouted, his voice cracking with fury, *"Tira abajo sus pistolas! A prisa!"*

"Yep, that's what he wants, all right."

As Suggs crouched and set his rifle on the ground, Longarm slowly lowered his hands, unbuckled his cartridge belt, and let it drop in the dust. When Suggs had dropped his own pistol belt, the lieutenant spewed more Spanish, wagging his pistol barrel between Longarm and Suggs as two of the young privates quickly swung down from their saddles.

"What's he sayin'?" Longarm asked Suggs.

"I ain't sure—he's speakin' too fast—but I think he wants to know if we have any more weapons on us."

The two privates gathered up the pistol belts, crouching down and glancing up at Longarm and Suggs as though

101

they were mountain lions, then scrambling back several feet as they slung the belts over their shoulders and leveled their carbines once more.

Longarm stared at the lieutenant and shook his head. "No! *No mas de las armas*. Any of you fellas speak English?"

The lieutenant stared at him. Slowly, his bushy, black brows smoothed out and his lips spread back from his large, yellow teeth, the roots protruding from the tobacco-stained gums. He rose up in his saddle, laughing as though at the funniest joke he'd ever heard. He looked at the younger *rurales* lined up on both sides of him. They all smiled. A couple of them laughed tensely.

Suddenly, the lieutenant stopped laughing and barked at the two *rurales* holding Longarm's and Suggs's cartridge belts. The two men leaped into action, hanging the belts over the horn of the lieutenant's saddle, then scrambled around behind the gringos and began patting them down.

"I don't think the lieutenant trusts you for shit, Custis," Suggs said, holding his hands to his shoulders and staring up at the *rurale* lieutenant.

"He don't look like he'd trust his mother with a peso's worth of chili peppers," Longarm said out of the side of his mouth as the private behind him slapped the sides of the lawman's dusty black frock.

He was glad when the soldier, missing the derringer in his vest pocket, continued on down to his legs and boots. He tensed when the younker rose from his haunches, patting his way back up to Longarm's vest.

The kid's right hand patted the right vest pocket. He grunted, froze. Longarm cursed under his breath. He looked down as the young *rurale*'s dirty brown hand slipped into his vest pocket and came out with the gold-plated derringer to which the end of the gold watch chain was attached.

The corporal held the derringer up above Longarm's right shoulder and rattled off some Spanish at the lieutenant, who glared down at Longarm, gritting his teeth, the flush rising once more under his Indian-dark skin. At the same time, the private who'd been patting down Suggs rose from his haunches. He held up an Arkansas toothpick he'd found in Suggs's right boot, and the .36 pocket pistol he'd plucked from the scout's right shin holster.

Longarm gave Suggs an admonishing look. "That's no way to win the man's trust, Lee."

"You should talk, Custis."

Huffing and blowing like an enraged bull caught in an ocotillo patch, the lieutenant swung down from his saddle, tossed his reins to the mounted corporal beside him, then stalked over to Suggs. He was raving like a warlock, spitting and showing his rotten teeth. As he approached Suggs, he cocked his right arm, holding the pistol in that hand, then swung the pistol butt forward.

It smacked against Suggs's right cheek, making Suggs's teeth clack. The old scout gave a yowl, stumbled back, twisting at the waist, and fell in the dirt.

The lieutenant jerked his enraged gaze to Longarm. He cocked his arm. As the gun butt came forward in the lieutenant's fist, Longarm ducked. As the fist whiffed over his head, Longarm buried his own right in the lieutenant's flat belly.

"Ugh!" the lieutenant cried.

Longarm straightened and delivered two smashing right uppercuts to the man's beaklike nose, blood spurting across his cheekbones. The man fell against his horse, but that's all Longarm saw before something hard slammed against the back of his head.

Everything went black.

Chapter 12

Longarm swam up through the pounding in his head to open his eyes.

The blazing sun shot arrows deep into his brain plate, so he kept them half-closed and lifted his chin from what it took him a moment to realize was a man's buckskin-clad shoulder. His chin tapped against the shoulder like a woodpecker pecking a cottonwood branch.

He rolled his eyes left, ran his gaze up from the sweat-soaked tunic collar and leathery, deep-lined neck to the pewter hair curling over a near-black, sun-spotted ear, then on up and forward to the profile of Lee Suggs. Below and forward, a horse's head bobbed, mane buffeting. The horse followed several gray-clad *rurales* in shaggy sombreros across a wide, flat, sage-spotted plain.

Dust hung in the winter-mild air like bits of gauze, dry and peppered with sage and creosote.

Longarm's butt hammered the dun's back, just back of Lee Suggs and the saddle. Each stride sent a miner's pick into Longarm's right ear as if it were being wielded by a crazy man certain he was about to chip into the mother lode.

Suggs turned his head slightly toward Longarm. His

lone eye was swelled nearly shut. "Rise and shine, sleeping beauty."

"Where the hell are we?"

"About five miles from the camp. Don't ask me where we're goin'. These Mescins talk way too fast for me to pick up much."

Longarm looked around. Two *rurales* rode off to his right, spread about twenty feet apart and sitting their trotting horses stiffly. Two more rode behind, holding their rifles across their saddle bows and eyeing Longarm blandly. One trailed Longarm's and the girl's saddled horses.

Longarm turned back to Suggs. "Where's Raquella?"

Suggs stared straight ahead. "She must've hid up in the rocks above the camp. They scoured the camp for another person. I told them Raquella's horse was just a spare, and maybe they finally believed me. Anyway, they didn't force the issue."

The scout chuckled dryly. "The lieutenant was about to drill a .44 slug through your head when he saw your wallet. It fell out on the ground when that private laid you out with his rifle stock, flashing your deputy U.S. marshal's badge. All I could make out from what they said was that they'd better bring us back to headquarters, let their superiors decide what to do with us."

Suggs glanced at him over his shoulder. "How is your head anyway?"

"Is it still on my shoulders?"

"Yeah."

"Could've fooled me."

Longarm looked around, and was about to ask Suggs if he thought there was any chance they might be able to shake free of this troupe, but let it go. On one horse, they'd never be able to outrun them, and even if they did, they'd have no weapons, water, or food.

That thought led to Raquella.

"They leave any food or water for the girl?"

Suggs shook his head.

Longarm looked over his shoulder, casting his worried gaze above the two *rurales* directly behind them to the low, blue buttes curving against the horizon.

The *rurales* stopped at sundown at what had once been an old peasant farm, half-buried in the sand of a vast playa at the base of a low, rocky hill over which salamanders flitted, flicking their tails. There was a ruined adobe house with a connecting barn and a screeching windmill, but since the buildings were uninhabitable, the *rurales*, Longarm, and Suggs bedded down amongst the rocks at the base of the butte.

Both of the *rurale* lieutenant's eyes were nearly swollen shut and he wore a bandage over his broken nose. He avoided the two prisoners all evening—except to cast an occasional, brooding glare at Longarm—as though they were carrying smallpox. Longarm and Suggs were given nothing to eat and only a sip of water before they bedded down in their blanket rolls.

Lying on his back, with his head against his saddle, Suggs fingered the swelling around his eye. "Custis, I'm gonna remember you in my will for breaking that greaser's nose."

"Yeah, but the joke's on me, ain't it?" Longarm's head felt like an exposed nerve, and only in the past hour had he begun to see less than double—somewhere around one and a half. Somehow, he and Suggs had to shake free of the *rurales*, go back and find Raquella, and get back after the Gatling guns.

He found no way to accomplish that within the next few hours. Still in the *rurales* net, they were up and riding with the next false dawn, after Longarm and Suggs had had to endure the smell of the *rurales*' beans, tortillas, and coffee without being offered anything except another tablespoon of water. Longarm and Suggs rode separately, their hands tied to their saddle horns, ankles lashed to their stirrups. They were quartering southeastward, the Black Widows rising on their right, looking like nothing if not the spiders they were named after—squat and black, with slopes and mesas extending like tentacles around their base, and streaked with low, smoky clouds.

Later that afternoon, the column traversed the shoulder of another in a long series of sun-washed, rocky hills in tabletop mesa country. As his bay, riding beside Suggs's dun, crested the rise and started down the other side, Longarm gazed into the broad canyon opening below.

A *pueblecito* sprawled at the bottom. Twenty or thirty adobe or sandstone dwellings capped with red or slate-gray roof tiles lay along both sides of the trail cleaving the town in two halves—one half sprawled at the base of a scrub-covered mountain on the right, the other fronting a broad creek trickling over rocks and winking in the waning sunlight. Several shawled women in colorful calico washed clothes along the bank of the creek, while three men in peasant garb were cutting down a dead pine on the other side.

Longarm and Suggs, riding in the middle of the ten-man *rurale* column, exchanged meaningful glances as they rode into the sprawling village. The air was rife with the smell of roasted, spicy meat, animal shit, and latrines. Chickens pecked in the dust between the cobblestones, while well-armed hombres milled outside the cantinas, some sitting around tables bedecked with tequila bottles, stone jugs, and shot glasses, while others lounged around the hitching posts.

Slow guitar music emanated from an upstairs window of one of the countless whorehouses.

One of the cholos, leaning against an awning post, muscular arms crossed on his chest, wore a two-foot-long, horn-handled knife on one thigh, a double-barreled shotgun on the other. As the column passed, the man grinned, showing a full set of silver-capped teeth as he yelled something at the lieutenant riding point. By the tone, he was ribbing the man about his broken nose. The lieutenant passed, keeping his head forward.

The procession continued along the street until, fifty yards ahead, the street widened and a vast, multilevel hacienda appeared on its right side. Set well back from the business district's hustle and bustle, it was a sprawling, red-tiled adobe with several large balconies and four or five massive sandstone chimneys gushing wood smoke from the different levels. A couple of dead pecan trees and a dry stone fountain stood in the center of the drive curving off the main drag and sweeping up in front of the curved stairs angling up to two oaken, iron-banded doors.

The place had obviously been the *pueblecito*'s center-piece at one time, probably inhabited by a wealthy landowner or high-level public official. Now, however, it had a slightly tumbledown air, with its cracked and bullet-pocked adobe. Several windows were missing shutters, and the paint on the remaining shutters was cracked and blistered. Leaves and tumbleweeds had blown up against the fountain and the house's front wall. Horse manure and straw littered the cobblestone driveway.

Several scruffy men—some dressed in worn *rurale* officer uniforms, others in the shabby suits and straw hats of small-town businessmen—sat about the patios, smoking and drinking. A couple of them had half-dressed women straddling their thighs or sprawled across their laps. One man, his uniform tunic open to reveal a grimy undershirt, sat on an adobe stair rail on the house's second story, leaning back against the wall with a beer bottle resting between his upraised knees, sound asleep.

The *rurale* column stopped before the hacienda, drawing semi-interested stares from the loungers on the patios and verandas. One man—portly, balding, and wearing only an undershirt and suspenders—nudged the bare-breasted young whore from his right knee and pushed himself to his feet. He staggered drunkenly to the wrought-iron rail before him and stared down at the column, his gaze quickly sweeping Longarm and Suggs before shuttling over to the lieutenant sitting his gray mare between the fountain and the house.

"Lieutenant Caddo," the fat man said, his Spanish slow enough for Longarm to follow, "why are you bringing those dirty gringos back to smell up my town? Did you run so low on ammunition that you couldn't *shoot* them?"

A couple of men on the balcony behind the fat man chuckled, one drawing the bare-breasted whore onto his own lap, the other pouring what looked like red wine or sangria into his beer mug.

Remaining mounted, the lieutenant produced Longarm's wallet from his tunic, held it out with the flap open, exposing the copper moon-and-star badge to the balcony. Roughly translated, he told the fat man that the tall "*bastardo* with the mustache" had possessed the U.S. marshal's badge.

The fat man frowned and gestured for the lieutenant to toss him the badge. The lieutenant threw it underhanded. The fat man's reactions were too slow, and the wallet clattered onto the cobbles. Angrily, the lieutenant ordered one of the privates to dismount and toss the wallet to the fat man, whom he called Captain Santangelo.

When the private had tossed the wallet successfully up to Santangelo, the fat man scrutinized it, his forearms resting on the rail before him, his gray, winglike brows beetled.

He tossed the wallet back down to the lieutenant and loosed a string of angry Spanish, then turned and sagged back down in his chair. Holding the wallet in one hand, the lieutenant dismounted and walked back toward Longarm and Suggs. He stopped just off Longarm's right stirrup, his bloodshot eyes glaring up at Longarm from their swollen sockets. His nose had ballooned up like a ripe plum.

110

He slipped his bone-handled bowie knife from its sheath on his cartridge belt with a flourish, then jabbed the point against the underside of Longarm's chin. The lawman winced at the poke.

The lieutenant gritted his teeth. In halting but intelligible English, he spat, "Capitán Santangelo requests the honor of your presence on the balcony." Then he lowered the knife and cut the ropes tying Longarm's wrists to the saddle horn.

As the lieutenant crouched to free the lawman's right foot from the stirrup, Longarm glanced at Suggs, who shrugged, said "Mexico," and shrugged again.

When Longarm and Suggs had dismounted, and the other *rurales* were leading their horses off around the side of the hacienda, the lieutenant clicked his heels together and gestured at the base of the stone steps rising to the balcony above. Rubbing his rope-chafed wrists, Longarm said, "What about our weapons?"

"Do not count your chickens before they are hatched, Señor." The lieutenant smiled, showing his rotten teeth and slitting his swollen eyes. "Besides, the *rurales* will protect you."

"Comforting," Longarm growled as he and Suggs started up the stairs, walking side by side, the lieutenant falling in behind them.

Longarm and Suggs stopped when they reached the balcony. Santangelo lounged in a wicker chair fifteen feet away, an unctuous smile on his mustachioed, unshaven face. There was a bottle on the table beside him.

Flanking the captain, several other men, two in *rurale* uniforms, played cards at a square table with stout wood legs. The round-faced girl who'd been sitting on Santangelo's lap now sat with one of the half-uniformed cardplayers, refilling the man's glass from a stone pitcher, while the other girl—full-hipped and wearing a short red dress and black corset, with red feathers in her coal-black hair—stood behind a man with lieutenant's bars on his shoulders, massaging the back of his neck as if to work out a stubborn knot.

The men and the two women glanced at Longarm and Suggs with only casual interest, and resumed their activities.

"Come, come, Señores," Santangelo said, gesturing at the wicker chair on his right and the high-backed dining room chair on his left. "Please sit, and let me apologize for Lieutenant Caddo's insolence. Sometimes the lieutenant is far too—how you say?—efficient for his own good."

"No real harm done," Suggs said, rubbing his bruised eye and glancing at the lieutenant behind them. "Caddo's the one breathin' through his mouth."

Santangelo grinned as he inspected the lieutenant's broken beak with obvious delight. "It serves you right, Caddo, for treating two such distinguished visitors—two U.S. *lawmen*—so shabbily." He raised his voice. "Leave us. You will head the next patrol first thing in the morning."

Lieutenant Caddo bunched his lips, flushing with indignation. *"Por favor, El Capitán—!"*

Santangelo loosed a barrage of angry Spanish as he rose half out of his chair, sending Caddo fairly sprinting back down the balcony stairs. When the lieutenant's boots had stopped clacking on the stones, Santangelo sank back down in his chair and announced resignedly, "He is my brother-in-law."

Longarm eased his tired butt into the wicker chair, while Suggs sat in the heavy, high-backed chair that had obviously been dragged out of a richly furnished dining room and treated poorly. "Actually, Captain," the lawman said, "Mr. Suggs is a U.S. Army scout. I'm the only lawman here. It was my own decision to pay this little unannounced visit to Mexico. Only I should be held responsible."

Suggs raised an eyebrow at him. Longarm ignored it.

"Ah, why so formal?" intoned Santangelo with exaggerated sadness. "Let us pour a drink for you each before we speak so seriously." He turned toward the cardplayers behind him and clapped his hands twice. In Spanish, he said, "Lenora, Marlena—pronto! I wish for the loveliest *putas* in Santa Luz to entertain my guests!"

The girls jumped with a start. They gathered beside the captain's chair, side by side, one covering her bare breasts with her hands, the one in the red skirt blushing and crossing one bare foot over the other, entwining her hands at her waist as her eyes flicked coquettishly between Longarm and the floor. Her right nipple peeked out between her fingers.

"Why so shy?" admonished the captain. "Lenora, entertain the yanqui marshal, as you seem to have chosen him already. Señor Suggs, may I introduce you to the lovely Marlena and the largest, firmest jugs in all of Santa Luz!"

The captain guffawed as the girls approached the gringos, shy as flower girls at a Catholic wedding. Marlena sat on Suggs's knee and snaked her hands around his neck as she asked him in Spanish if he liked Mexican girls. Suggs chuckled nervously. "Well, yes . . . but then I reckon there ain't many girls I *don't* like!"

The younger, slimmer Lenora approached Longarm's chair, and knelt beside him. She placed her hands on the right arm of the chair, rested her chin on her knuckles, and looked up at him nearly without expression from beneath her thin, black brows. She had a pretty, heart-shaped face. She couldn't have been much over fourteen, and the small, pale scar on her chin, shaped like a half-moon, did nothing to mar her beauty.

"I hope the señoritas will not be too distracting," Santangelo said, filling a cracked goblet from a brown bottle on the table beside him, then extending the goblet to Suggs. "I thought they would compliment the pulque—a

113

local specialty brewed by our undertaker—in cutting the dust from your throat as well as atone for your inexcusably poor treatment by Lieutenant Caddo."

Reaching for the glass the captain offered him, Longarm sat back in his chair and glanced at the girl. "Poor treatment? Captain, I don't know what you're talking about."

Santangelo laughed and, holding his own drink between the thumb and index finger of his right hand, crossed his legs. He was barefoot, his pudgy feet etched with large purple veins, the toenails thick and hard as seashells.

"Now then, getting down to business," he said, a hard light flashing in his eyes as he leveled his gaze on Longarm, "tell me what brings you to Méjico *por favor*."

Chapter 13

Longarm saw no reason to dance around Captain Santangelo's question.

"Three brand-new Gatling guns," he said as the young *puta*, Lenora, sat on the floor before his chair and rubbed her cheek against his knee. He blocked the girl's sensual caresses out of his mind and added, "Stolen off an ambushed Army supply train near San Angelo, Texas."

"Who stole your guns, Señor?" the captain asked blandly, staring down at his bare foot.

"Soldiers on the train reported seeing Yaquis—or people who they thought were Yaquis. It was night."

As the bare-breasted whore, Marlena, leaned back against Suggs's chest and stared into space with a bored air, he said, "A patrol was sent out after the train robbers. They were ambushed by Yaquis. Only one man survived—the commanding officer of Fort Sabre."

"We were trailing a couple of bronco Yaquis, and shaking ourselves free of border bandits, when your Lieutenant Caddo caught up to us." Longarm sipped the pulque, to which the undertaker had no doubt added a liberal portion of coffin varnish. It seared the lawman's tonsils and put a kink in his windpipe, like a strong whiff of ammonia. In a pinched voice, he continued. "The Yaquis were heading toward the Black Widow Mountains. We'd hoped they'd lead us to the Gatlings. . . ."

"*Sí, sí,*" said Santangelo, sighing as he wiggled his bare foot. "And then Lieutenant Caddo entered the picture and spoiled everything." He clucked admonishingly as he shuttled his gaze between Longarm and Suggs. "You might have given my government the courtesy of explaining your intentions, Señores. You know as well as I that your country does not allow officials of the mejicano government to cross the Rio Bravo and ride north into Texas. How is it that you, officials of the *American* government, felt justified in crossing the Rio Grande and heading into Méjico?"

Suggs opened his mouth to respond, his brows furrowed angrily, but Longarm cut him off. "We were wrong to do so, Captain Santangelo. And we beg your forgiveness. I offer no excuses, only an explanation. It would have taken an inordinate amount of time to arrange a proper border crossing with the Mexican government. By the time we could have done so, those Gatling guns might have been used on more of our soldiers, or on the good citizens of Mexico. Possibly your own *rurales*. While we have no idea what the Yaquis want with those guns, I'll bet you pesos to pinto beans they don't intend to use them for target practice."

"Ahh," said the captain, nodding slowly. "Your point is well taken, Marshal Long. While I cannot condone your actions—as your government would not condone mine if our positions were reversed—I see how it would be in *both* our country's interests to retrieve those guns."

Suggs slid a breeze-blown lock of Marlena's hair from his cheek. "That mean you'll help us? If we set out first thing tomorrow on fresh horses—with, say, ten or twelve experienced shooters and riders, and with two weeks worth of grub—we'd be in the Black Widows in two days."

Captain Santangelo slid his pensive gaze from Longarm to Suggs, and pooched out his lips. "Let me think about it overnight, uh? Even with a contingent of thirty-three men here in Santa Luz, I am very short-handed. If I am not running down the savage Apache, I am scouring the hills for cattle rustlers and *bandidos*. As it is, with three patrols out, I have only eleven men here at the hacienda."

Santangelo shook his head. "No, let me think about it. In the meantime, let me invite you back here for dinner and drinks, perhaps a little poker and music, after siesta." Santangelo grinned. "In the meantime, the girls will show you to their rooms to relax, uh?"

Santangelo rose stiffly. He barked orders in Spanish to the girls, shook hands with Longarm and Suggs, then turned, sauntered past the cardplayers, a couple of whom cast Longarm and the scout indignant glances, then into the house through a broad, open doorway.

Lenora took Longarm's hand in both her own, and gave it a tug, staring up at him coolly. At the same time, Marlena giggled and began leading Suggs toward the same door through which the captain had disappeared.

Suggs shrugged at Longarm, and followed the girl past the cardplayers and into the house.

"Come on, Marshal Long," Lenora said in Spanish. "Do not be shy."

The cardplayers grumbled as Longarm let himself be led past the table and into the chilly shadows of the hacienda. The place still showed signs of its original opulence— heavy wooden furniture and gilt wall hangings—but it had been turned into a *rurale* barracks, with desks and cots and gun cabinets. Tobacco smoke and filled slop buckets permeated the air, and low Spanish voices echoed down dark corridors.

The girl led Longarm through a maze of rooms and stone-floored hallways, through a courtyard, up a winding staircase littered with mouse shit and cigarette butts, and into another dim hall with heavy wooden doors on both sides in arched frames. He'd taken only a few steps when

Suggs materialized from the shadows to fall into step beside him. Marlena's thin shadow moved several yards ahead.

"What do you think about this, Custis?" the scout said softly as he and Longarm moved down the hall, Lenora still tugging on the lawman's arm.

"Never thought I'd say this in such a situation, but I don't like it. Santangelo doesn't strike me as a straight talker."

"Yeah, I get the feelin' he's up to somethin'. What—I don't know."

"I've yet to meet a *rurale* I'd trust as far as I could throw him into a Sonoran sandstorm."

They strode a few more steps in silence. Suggs stopped, turned to Longarm. "Wanna make a break for it, steal a couple of horses?"

As Longarm stopped, the girl turned to him and tugged on his arm, urging him forward. Longarm held his ground and said, "I thought of that. Scratched it. I've been hearing boot clomps behind us. We gained an extra shadow."

He and Suggs turned to glance behind them. A bulky silhouette filled the far end of the arched hall. A cigar coal glowed in the dimness, reflected on the barrel of the rifle the man held across his chest.

Down the opposite end of the hall, Marlena called in Spanish, "Come, Señor Suggs. My room is *this* way!"

Suggs turned a wan smile on Longarm. "I reckon I could use a siesta after all. And I wouldn't want to break the young lady's heart."

He and Longarm strode forward. As they approached the door on the hall's left side, which Lenora was opening, Suggs leaned close to whisper in Longarm's ear, "Be careful you don't get a stiletto in the back, my friend."

He continued down the hall.

Longarm stopped and began moving through the door Lenora had opened, grumbling, "You too."

He stopped halfway into the room and stuck his head back into the hall. At the far end, the cigar coal glowed deep umber, the rich smell of the stogie spicing the air. Longarm pulled his head into the room and closed the door.

The room was as dim as the hall, as there was only one window, too small for a man to crawl through. Lenora struck a match and lit a lamp on a clothes chest. By the light of the flickering flame, Longarm saw a small four-poster bed covered with a red and yellow quilt, a small writing desk, a straight-back chair, and a washstand with an enamel basin. A small wooden crucifix hung on the wall over the bed.

The girl spread her arms across the top of the clothes chest behind her, and planted one bare foot atop the other. A thick wing of her blue-black hair fell across one plump cheek. "How you like to do it, hombre?"

Longarm had the *rurales*, the Yaquis, and Raquella on his mind. He was in no mood for horsing around.

He doffed his hat, and tossed it over a bedpost. "Boy, am I tired! You don't mind if I just take a nap, do you, Lenora?" He lay down on the bed, letting his boots hang over the end, and crossed his hands behind his head.

The girl slowly lowered her arms from the chest, frowning. "You don't like me?"

"It ain't that."

"I must please you, Señor, or the captain will send me back home." Lenora shook her head vehemently. "I do not want to go *home*! The captain says I must please or go back to my uncle. . . ."

She moved away from the chest, crossed her arms, and lifted her dress over her head in one swift movement. She tossed the dress onto the chair and stood before him, brown and sleek and beautiful, breasts like small, olive-colored cantaloupes.

"How you like?" she whispered as she moved to the bed

and slowly sank down on top of him, kissing him softly, then burying her face in his chest. She took a deep sniff, then kissed his throat, and he felt her warm hands on his crotch, opening his fly.

He ran his hands down her long, smooth back. At least she doesn't have a stiletto on her, he thought as she scuttled down his body and stuck her warm, wet tongue through his open fly. When it touched his stiffening shaft, he sighed.

And she wasn't as inexperienced as she looked.

He let her work him with her tongue for a time. Then he placed his hands on her fragile shoulders and pulled her head up to his, kissed her rose-petal lips. He lowered his head to her chest and suckled her breasts, the nipples pebbling under his tongue as he ran his hands down her firmly curving buttocks and along the cool backs of her thighs.

Finally, he turned her over on the bed, got up, kicked off his boots, and shucked out of his clothes. Naked, he walked back to the bed, shaft jutting before him. The girl scuttled toward him on the bed, rose up on her hands and knees, and wrapped her hand around his cock, pumping him gently. She looked up at him, smiled, then closed her mouth over the bulging head of his shaft until he felt the hot, narrow back of her throat. Her tongue snaked around him, lubricating him with her warm saliva.

She pulled her mouth away, spittle stringing between her mouth and his throbbing member. With an eager grunt, she lay back on the bed, lifted her feet, spread her legs, and grinned.

He eased onto the bed and crawled up between her legs, mounting her, and lowered his mouth to hers. As his tongue slipped between her lips, his cock cleaved the warm, slick lobes of her snatch.

"Madre de Dios!" she whispered and closed her legs around his back, pressing her heels against his hips. She wrapped her arms around his neck, hugging him tightly. "Oh, *Madre de Dios*!"

He pulled out, thrust back in, and continued the maneuver until the bed was sighing and squawking and slamming against the wall and the girl was thrashing and crying out beneath him, her bent legs flapping like wings.

At last, she turned her head sideways and stretched her lips back from her teeth, eyes tightly closed. He locked his hands over hers, spread her arms straight out to the sides of the bed, bucked forward, and groaned as his seed rocketed into her core.

When he finished, he fell sideways on the bed, fatigued by all the aches and pains and hard desert miles. He closed his eyes, and sleep washed over him like floodwater over a dam.

Longarm wasn't sure how much time had passed when he opened his eyes. He lay on the girl's bed, staring up at the herringbone-patterned ceiling. The girl was gone, though the indentation of her body was visible in the mattress to Longarm's right.

The lamp had burned low, and no light penetrated the small window above his head. The room was nearly dark. Silence, except for a mule braying far off in the hills and the breeze sweeping foliage beyond the window. There was the smell of coal oil from the lamp and of cook fires from the window.

With a tired groan, Longarm dropped his bare feet to the stone floor, took a deep breath, then stood, washed at the basin, and dressed. He went out into the hall lit by three small candles in a wall sconce, and looked around, half-expecting the big rifleman to still be standing sentinel at the hall's far end.

The arched doorway was empty.

Longarm walked down to Marlena's room, and knocked. No answer. He knocked again and leaned close to listen.

"Suggs?"

He pushed the latch down, pushed the door open. By the candlelight washing in around him, he saw that the room was empty, the bed rumpled.

He closed the door and strode down the hall, turned left at the end. A boot clicked on the flagstones beside him, and something round and cold jabbed his head, just behind his ear.

"Enjoy the *puta*, Señor?" said a raspy Spanish voice off his right shoulder.

Longarm froze, back tensing. "Talented girl."

The man chuckled. There was the snick-click of a revolver being cocked, and the barrel moved against Longarm's head. "Straight ahead, gringo. *Vamonos*!"

Chapter 14

Longarm did as he was told, and started down the hall. He glanced over his shoulder. The man behind him, aiming a cocked Schofield at his spine, was a skinny, long-haired hombre with wide-spaced eyes and a corporal's insignia on his sleeves. He grinned evilly.

"Where are we going?" Longarm asked in Spanish.

"Shut up!" the Mexican barked in English.

They walked through the cavernlike barracks for nearly ten minutes before they came to a pair of stout, iron-banded oak doors. The corporal opened the right door, ordered Longarm through. A wooden staircase dropped into flickering shadows and wan torchlight.

Slowly, Longarm descended the curving stairs into what looked like an old storeroom. The dank air was musty, tinged with the sweet smell of wine and burning tar from the three torches leaning out from the cracked adobe walls.

Two young *rurales* sat on either side of three stacked crates stamped PEACHES, just left and in front of another stout oak door. They had their shirts off, and they were arm wrestling, the leaner of the two slowly lowering the beefier lad's hand toward the table. The corporal behind Longarm ordered one of the men to unlock the door.

Grumbling, the young *rurales* halted their match, and the beefy younker stood heavily, picked a corn-husk cigarette from an ashtray, and stuck it in his mouth. He grabbed a stout key off a peg by the door, stuck the key in the lock.

Seconds later, Longarm found himself striding down a row of iron-banded cells lit by a couple more wall flares, the corporal maintaining a six-foot gap behind him. There were four cells on each side of the narrow corridor, set deep within pillared porticos.

Three cells on the left were occupied by obvious *bandidos*. Only one cell on the right was occupied—the second one down. Lee Suggs sat on one of the cell's two cots, elbows on his knees, a cigarette in his right hand, his battered Stetson beside him on the cot.

He looked up as Longarm approached, his face a grisly mask with the blind right eye and the swollen left one. It was hard to tell on such a face, but the old scout appeared to wear no expression whatever.

The corporal opened the door, shoved Longarm inside. Longarm turned as the corporal slammed the door and twisted the key in the lock.

"You wanna tell me what this is all about?"

The corporal pulled the key from the lock and glared between the bars. "Shut up, gringo!" His voice echoed off the thick, adobe walls as he turned and strode back down the corridor.

When the stout door at the end of the corridor squawked open, then slammed shut, Longarm turned to Suggs, who was drawing on his cigarette. "Welcome to Mexico," the scout said, blowing out a long smoke plume.

Longarm looked around. There were no windows. The only furnishing besides the cots was a tin slop bucket. He turned to Suggs. "What are we doin' here, hoss?"

"Your guess is as good as mine. Fickle bastard, Santangelo. Let's us fuck and sleep, then throws us in the hoosegow." His beard rose as he smiled. "Gotta admit, I ain't had my ashes hauled like that in a long time."

Longarm stood in front of the door. "Think he's got the Gatlings?"

Suggs shook his head as he leaned back against the wall and hiked his boot onto the edge of the cot. "I think he just wants to impress his superiors by having collared a U.S. lawman and an Army scout on Mex soil. Or maybe he's just a typical crazy *rurale* hooked on pulque and power. He'll let us molder here a good, long time before sending us home . . . with his sincere apologies for the shabby treatment."

"What about the guns?"

"I don't think he gives a shit about the guns. If he even believes our story. Maybe he thinks you stole that badge off a marshal you killed. Maybe we're headin' for a stash of stolen gold in the Sierra Madre."

Longarm sagged down on his own cot, leaned back against the wall, and rested one arm on an upraised knee. "Got any other theories?"

"Those are about it."

"Good." Longarm pulled a cheroot from his shirt pocket. "You been in here longer than me. Figure a way out yet?"

"Nope."

Longarm cursed and lit his cigar. The thick walls didn't allow for much noise to penetrate the cellar, so Longarm and the scout sat smoking, listening to only the occasional ceiling creak or muffled thump. Soft snores rose from one of the cells, echoing off the walls.

Around ten o'clock, the door to the cell block opened and the beefier of the two arm wrestlers appeared, fully dressed now, a key ring in one hand. He walked down the corridor, peering into the cells. He stopped at Longarm and Suggs's cell, glanced through the bars, then began to turn back the other way.

Longarm said, "Tell Captain Santangelo I want to see him."

The guard wrinkled his nose, turned away, and strode back down the corridor and out the door.

Suggs sighed. "Relax, Custis. Get some more sleep, see what tomorrow brings."

He smashed his cigarette stub out on the floor, then lay down on the cot and tipped his hat over his eyes. In less than a minute, long snores rose from his fluttering lips, and his belly, over which his buckskin tunic stretched taut, rose and fell evenly.

Longarm chuckled dryly, and took another puff off his cigar. One of the other prisoners chattered quietly in his sleep. Another began snoring. Longarm finished the cigar, stubbed out the butt, and lay down. He stared at the cracked ceiling until the torches burned out, cloaking the cell in dank darkness.

He remembered now why he hated Mexico. It was all smoke and mirrors down here.

He closed his eyes and tried willing himself to sleep. Fatigue from all the aches and pains made his chest and limbs heavy, and his head was still sore from the clubbing, but sleep would not wash over him.

Finally, with a frustrated sigh, he swung his feet back to the floor and reached into his coat for another cheroot. A muffled pop sounded above the echoing snores. A man screamed on the other side of the heavy oak door, and then the gun popped again.

Longarm left his three remaining cigars in his inside coat pocket. He stood, walked over to the cell door, and angled a look through the soupy darkness on the left.

Behind him, Suggs chuckled in his sleep, sighed deeply, then continued sawing logs.

At the far end of the hall, a key clattered in a lock. Door hinges squawked, and a dull, buttery glow appeared. The light moved slowly from side to side, silhouetting the figure behind it. The man moved along the corridor, holding the lamp high in his right hand, turning to peer into each cell, his boots clicking softly on the flagstones. The light reflected off the rifle he held low in his left fist.

As the lamp and the man approached Longarm's cell, the figure behind and below the light materialized from the darkness. The lamp went up another few inches, illuminating thick, black hair and lustrous, brown eyes. Raquella stared through the bars from beneath the brim of her ratty sombrero.

"Marshal Long?"

"Jesus Christ," Longarm rasped. "How in the hell did you get in here?"

"Shh! We must not wake the other prisoners."

She lowered the lamp and stuck the key in the lock with an echoing rattle and clang. Behind Longarm, Suggs's snores died abruptly. The scout grunted, and his cot creaked. "What the—?"

Longarm and the girl shushed him at the same time.

As Raquella swung the door open, Suggs came up off the cot, his hat in his hand, and strode up beside Longarm at the door. He whispered, "How in the hell did she get in here?"

"Stop asking questions and follow me," Raquella whispered, moving back down the corridor, holding the lamp high in her hand.

Longarm grabbed his own hat, and he and Suggs followed her down the corridor, walking softly on the balls of their feet as one of the prisoners continued snoring and another continued muttering. Raquella had left the main door ajar. She pushed through it, her lamp casting shadows around the small room in the middle of which stood the three peach crates with a deck of cards on top. The two guards lay sprawled on the floor around the table, one facedown, knees curled toward his chest, the other on his back.

"Nice work," Suggs said, moving into the room behind Longarm.

"Quickly!" Raquella headed for the stone steps rising toward the second story. "These walls are thick, but someone might have heard the shots."

"Hold on."

Longarm grabbed the lamp out of her hand, held it over the two dead guards as he reached down and pulled the pistol from the skinny guard's covered holster. He tossed the Schofield to Suggs, then grabbed the other guard's bone-gripped Remington. Shoving the Remy behind his waistband, he spied two trapdoor Spencer rifles leaning against the far wall.

He grabbed one and tossed it to Suggs, who levered the cocking mechanism to make sure it was loaded. Longarm grabbed the other Spencer, and set the lamp on the table. Checking his own rifle for loads, he moved past Raquella toward the bottom of the stone steps.

At the top, a latch clicked. Longarm ducked into the shadows beside the stairs, Raquella and Suggs following suit. The girl hunkered down beside Longarm, a New Line .41 revolver in her right fist.

A voice called in Spanish, "Miguel, Pancho—everything all right down there?"

Longarm looked over Raquella's head at Suggs. In the darkness, he could see only the scout's pearl-gray eye staring back at him tensely. He turned forward as boots clacked on the steps, the footfalls growing louder and faster. The voice echoed in the stairwell, pitched with exasperation: "Miguel? Pancho? What is—"

Longarm reached up and closed his hand around the man's left ankle. The man yowled as he tumbled headfirst down the stairs. He landed on a shoulder and rolled, arms and legs flailing, unbuttoned uniform tunic flapping at his sides.

Longarm bolted out from the side of the stairs. The man

lay in a heap at the bottom. As he pushed up on his hands, his smashed lips bloody, his shiny black eyes found Longarm.

It was the long-haired corporal who'd led him down here. The man opened his mouth to scream, but Longarm stopped him by ramming the toe of his right cavalry boot against the underside of the corporal's chin.

The man's head snapped back with an audible crack. He flew back over his heels and piled up in the corner. The thick fetor of raw alcohol emanated from the man's still body.

Suggs and the girl ran out from the shadows beside the stairs. Longarm held his left hand up, palm out, staring up the steps, listening.

Through the open door at the top of the stairs he could hear a din, muffled by distance, including what sounded like mariachi music. None of the other *rurales* seemed to be at this end of the hacienda.

"Let's go!" Holding the Spencer in his right hand, Longarm bolted up the steps. He slowed at the top, gently shoved the half-open door wide, shuttling his gaze left and right along the broad, candlelit hall.

The din of men shouting and women laughing amidst the music of a mariachi band echoed down the left corridor. As Raquella and Suggs stepped into the hall, Longarm glanced at the girl. "Which way?"

"I tied three horses on the other side of the main street." She brushed past him, moving left down the hall, holding her revolver barrel up in her right hand. "We go this way."

Suggs glanced at Longarm. "Think she found the Gatlings for us too?"

"Wouldn't put it past her." Longarm ran after the girl, stopped when Spanish exclamations rose behind him. He and Suggs wheeled at the same time.

Two *rurale* privates stood at the corner of an intersecting corridor, scrambling to bring up their old Springfield

129

rifles hanging from lanyards looped over their right shoulders. Longarm and Suggs fired at almost the same time, the reports echoing like cannon fire in the adobe-lined hall.

Throwing their rifles above their heads, both privates were punched back by the bullets tearing through their chests. They screamed and hit the floor with soft thuds and the rattle of spur chains. The one on the right lay still; the other shouted angrily, face twisted with pain, and reached for his revolver.

Suggs drilled another round through his forehead, laying him out dead.

"Shit!" Longarm barked as he stared at the two dead *rurales* through the wafting gun smoke. His ears rang from the rifle reports, which had no doubt been heard by every man in the hacienda.

"Vamos!" Raquella called behind him, beckoning furiously. "There is only one outside door on this end! We must get to it before the other *rurales* do!"

Racking fresh shells in their Spencers' breeches, Longarm and Suggs turned and ran after the girl.

"I don't think we was s'posed to come down here and kill *rurales*, Custis!" Suggs said as they ran around the corner, past a statue of a robed saint holding a sparrow in one hand, and lit off down another corridor, heading toward the front of the hacienda.

"What were we supposed to do?" Longarm said. "Wrestle 'em down and tickle 'em?"

The girl ran about twenty yards ahead, her wool poncho buffeting around her bare, brown thighs, thick hair flapping on her shoulders. Occasional torches burned from wall brackets, casting spheres of guttering light between long stretches of deep shadow.

Exasperated voices rose around them, echoing. Someone was furiously shouting orders.

Suddenly, Raquella stopped, staring straight ahead. Longarm held up to her left. "What is it?"

She didn't have to answer. Three silhouettes were running toward them, fifty yards off down the hall and closing.

"There a back door?" Longarm asked.

"I don't know."

Suggs said, "We best check!"

As they turned to run back the other way, they froze once more. Four more silhouettes ran toward them from the hall's other end, shouting and cursing and loudly racking shells into rifle breeches.

"You made too much noise!" Raquella scolded. She added with a resigned air, "We are surrounded. . . ."

Chapter 15

"Mierda!" one of the *rurales* up the hallway cursed. *"Los gringos!"*

"Shit!" Suggs yelled, jerking his head around to peer both up the hall and down. "We got us a shootin' match!"

Longarm drew a quick bead on one of the four *rurales* bearing down on him with a Winchester from up the corridor, and fired. His slug sparked along the man's extended rifle, ricocheted off the rear stock, and punched into the side of the head of the man to his right. It blew the *rurale*'s sombrero off and threw him against the wall.

The man's scream hadn't died before both Suggs and Raquella opened up on the three men approaching from down the hall. As Longarm racked another load and snapped the Spencer up, men screamed and shouted ahead of and behind him, pistol and rifle fire exploding and echoing like thunder in a deep canyon.

Slugs chopped into the stone floor and the adobe walls, spanging as they echoed, adobe slivers flying in all directions.

Longarm fired two more shots at the *rurales* shouting and scrambling in front of him. One who'd just dropped to his knee and raised an old Krag rifle to his shoulder was spun around by Longarm's slug. The man bounced his rifle off the wall and fell, groaning and clutching his side.

The remaining two *rurales* fired at the same time on opposite sides of the corridor. One round tore out the seam in Longarm's right jacket shoulder, while the other whistled across his left cheek and slammed into the wall behind him.

Longarm dropped the Spencer, plucked the Remington revolver from behind his waistband, and dove against the right wall and under two more whistling bullets. Lying belly-down against the cold stone floor, he raised the Remington and began firing, not stopping until both *rurales* lay groaning and the Remington's hammer clicked on a spent casing.

On the far side of the hall, Raquella squeezed off a shot from behind an empty clay pot, aiming down the corridor. On one knee, Suggs triggered his Spencer. The bullets chopped into stone and adobe, ricocheting wildly into the distant shadows. A man screamed. Boots clattered on the flagstones. The silhouette of one running *rurale* dwindled down the hall, beyond two figures sprawled on the floor, and darted out of sight around a corner.

Longarm whipped another look up the corridor. A foyer framing a stout wooden door was on the left, about thirty yards away. Beyond it up the hall, more boots clattered and men yelled. He recognized the enraged voice of Santangelo.

"Let's go!" Longarm shouted, pushing off his heels and bolting up the hall. He leaped over one of the men he'd shot, stopped, and whipped back around as Suggs and Raquella ran past him.

"Come on, Custis!" Suggs said. "There's more on the way!"

Longarm reached down, picked up a rifle, ran his hand down the forestock marked with fresh scratches and speckled with glistening blood drops. "Found my rifle!"

"Well, take it and let's go!"

Longarm quickly unbuckled the cartridge belt of the dead man in front of him, slung it over his shoulder. Hefting his Winchester in one hand, he ran after Suggs and the girl, who was swerving toward the door. Beyond, bobbing silhouettes took shape. A gun flashed in the near darkness, followed by the echoing report. The bullet careened past Longarm and skidded along the wall.

He dropped to one knee and hammered six shots into the shadows, then bolted through the open door. On a leaf-littered portico, he tripped over a boot, nearly fell. The girl was crouched to his left, peering around the edge of the wide door casing. Suggs was doing the same on the right.

Longarm looked down, saw the *rurale* sergeant slumped against a mesquite shrub, legs extended across the step. His pants and underwear were bunched around his ankles, and his throat had been slit from ear to ear.

Longarm glanced at Raquella, frowning.

"He was guarding the door," she said matter-of-factly. "I offered him a blow job for a peso, but he bought a slit throat instead."

"Good girl," said Suggs wryly.

Boots and shouted epithets grew louder in the hall behind them.

Longarm looked around. They were at the front of the hacienda, at one of three or four doors, with most of the building stretching to the right. A patio of cracked flagstones and dead shrubs lay before them, surrounded by a low stone wall. A doorway that no longer had a door in it lay on the other side. Beyond lay the dry fountain. Beyond the fountain, the torch-lit street where night revelers milled amidst a perpetual, muffled din.

"Which way are the horses from here?" Longarm asked Raquella.

"Straight across the street, at the end of an alley."

"Let's go."

Longarm bolted straight across the patio and through the open doorway. He stepped to the right as Raquella and Suggs ran through behind him. Raquella hunkered down beside Longarm. Suggs was breathing hard, and he was favoring his left foot.

"You hit?" Longarm asked him.

Suggs pressed his back to the opposite side of the wall, holding his cocked pistol across his chest. "A bullet creased my ankle's all."

"Keep going," Longarm rasped. He fired a shot across the patio, where a shadow and a gun barrel flickered in the doorway they'd just left. "I'll meet you on the main street."

Suggs turned and jogged, grunting as he limped on his right foot across the paved drive and into the shadows between the hacienda and the main street. Longarm glanced at the girl on one knee beside him.

"You too."

She stared at him a moment, then grabbed his forearm, leaned forward, and kissed him. "Hurry. I stole the horses, and the *bandidos* they belong to will be looking for them soon."

With that, she jumped up and ran after Suggs, her silhouette quickly melding with the night shadows. Longarm stared wonderingly after her, the sensation of her soft lips lingering on his own.

A rifle popped and flashed twice in the hacienda's open door. As Santangelo shouted orders behind them, two men bolted onto the patio, triggering pistols. Another ran out levering a Winchester. The bullets exploded against the patio wall, ricocheting and spraying adobe.

Longarm snaked his Winchester through the wall's opening and fired three quick shots. One of the *rurales* went down while the other two shouted angrily and opened up on Longarm. He pressed his back against the wall, gritting his teeth against the fusillade.

A hammer clacked on an empty shell, and then the

other gun fell silent as well. Longarm snaked his Winchester through the opening once more and emptied it, the smoke and darkness preventing him from seeing what he hit. But he could hear a muffled grunt and the soft thumps of bodies smacking the flagstones.

As the last shell casing rattled onto the gravel behind him, he bolted up and forward and lit out across the hacienda's paved drive, which curved off toward the right. Lights still glittered on the broad balcony where he and Suggs had sat with Santangelo only hours ago, and where, apparently, the *rurales* had been celebrating heartily until all had broken loose. The aroma of roasted javelina wafted in the cool night air.

As Longarm ran along the side of a stone building, heading for the main street and keeping to the shadows left of the paved drive, he stretched a glance behind him. Three men ran out of the hacienda's main entrance while two more ran down a long, curving staircase dropping from the broad balcony.

He could hear Santangelo screaming and shouting madly while a couple of pistols popped feebly from the direction of the patio.

Longarm continued running, hurdling trash and what was left of an old, two-wheeled hay cart. When he got to the front of the stone hovel, he turned left onto the main street. He stopped under a brush arbor, hunkered down, laid his rifle across his knees, began filling it from the cartridge belt hanging off his left shoulder, and looked around.

Silhouettes capped with sombreros lined the boardwalks, apparently drawn out of the hog pens and cantinas by the gunfire emanating from the *rurale* compound. None of the charros or vaqueros seemed to want anything to do with the trouble, however. They stood around under the brush arbors, silhouetted by torch and lantern light, talking and holding glasses and cigars in their hands. A couple of

137

them held laughing women. Guitar music spilled from a dimly lit cantina somewhere off to Longarm's left.

The pre-Christmas revelry continued.

Someone whistled. Longarm angled his glance across the street.

An arm beckoned from a dark alley mouth. Longarm slid the last cartridge into the Winchester's loading door, stood, jacked a fresh shell into the chamber, and lurched forward off the boardwalk. He ran across the street, turned around horses clumped at a hitch rack, and paused at the mouth of the dark alley between two cantinas. He felt dark eyes watching him from both sides. The aromatic smoke of Mexican tobacco mingled with raw liquor and horse manure.

Down the alley, shadows moved, dwindling into the darkness. There was the ping of a boot kicking a tin can.

Longarm glanced over his right shoulder. Two men in dove-gray, one wearing a sombrero, one hatless, ran out from around the stone building across the street. Rifles held at port, they jerked their heads around.

As Longarm bolted forward down the alley, one of the *rurales* yelled and triggered a shot. The bullet tore into the corner of the cantina as Longarm sprinted off through the shadows, leaping trash, brush, and rocks. A cat meowed to his left, giving him a momentary start before it hunkered low atop a crate pile, back humped, eyes glittering at him in the darkness.

As Longarm made the end of the alley, Suggs yelled, "Custis!"

He came to a skidding halt and turned to his left. Suggs and the girl were on two horses with silver-mounted saddles and bridles. Suggs tossed the reins of a third mount—a grulla with two white stockings—at Longarm.

The old scout said, just loud enough for Longarm to hear, "Let's split the wind, though how we're gonna find our way in the dark, I don't know!"

"I know the country," Raquella said, reining her horse around. "Follow me!"

Longarm grabbed the horn and toed a stirrup. As he swung the grulla around, the two *rurales* bolted out of the alley. In Spanish, one yelled what Longarm translated as "Hold it, gringo, or I fill you full of holes!"

Longarm extended the Winchester in one hand and triggered a shot, then ground his heels into the grulla's flanks. He headed south after Suggs and the girl, toward the creek glistening silver in the darkness. Behind him, the *rurales* triggered several shots, all sparking off rocks or blowing up gravel at the grulla's lunging rear hooves.

The *rurales* were probably better shots when they were sober. Longarm was glad he'd caught them in a celebratory mood.

The grulla splashed through the shallow creek, its shod hooves clacking on the rocks, then pushed up the opposite bank and lunged into a steady lope across a wide, brushy flat. Longarm didn't like running a horse in the darkness, which risked killing both him and the horse, but Raquella was setting a fast pace. He hoped she knew the country as well as she seemed, and didn't run them all into a miner's diggings or an abandoned well.

As they pushed across the valley and began climbing into low, gray hills, he glanced back several times. Nothing behind him but sifting dust, darkness, and the soft, twinkling lights of Santa Luz.

He was about to slide his Winchester into the boot beneath his right leg when he noticed the boot was already carrying a Sharps. For the first time, he inspected the well-trimmed bridle and saddle, its large, Spanish-style horn glistening with gold stitching.

"Hey, where'd you get these horses?" he called to the girl now trotting her steeldust just ahead and right.

"I stole them from *bandidos* fornicating in a brothel at the edge of town." Raquella turned to him, her teeth showing white between her lips. "It is not a sin to steal from sinners, eh?"

Suggs was riding left of Longarm. "Why'd you come for us, Señorita? You sure didn't have to risk your pretty neck for us two reprobates."

"You saved my hide, so I saved yours." Raquella glanced at Longarm, then glanced away. "Besides, we are partners, no?"

Longarm said, "How'd you know where we were?"

"I ran down a horse outside the canyon, and followed you." She turned to him again, but he couldn't see her face in the darkness. "Now, you help me find my sister, right?"

"You got it."

Raquella heeled her horse into a lope.

Chapter 16

Longarm, Suggs, and Raquella pushed hard for an hour, loping, then trotting the horses through the starlit darkness. Longarm dropped back several times and scouted their back trail, surprised to find that the *rurales* were not behind them.

"They're probably thinking the Yaqui'll do their jobs for them," Suggs grunted. "And they're probably right."

They continued riding until three o'clock in the morning, trying to put as much ground between them and Santa Luz as they could, then dry-camped in a narrow canyon concealed on three sides by steep rock walls. Once they'd tended the horses, staking them in oak grass, they spread out around the west side of the canyon, collapsing beneath their blankets, resting their heads against the *bandidos'* silver-mounted saddles.

At dawn, they breakfasted on frijoles, canned tomatoes, and the dried rabbit Raquella had found in the grub sack tied to her saddle horn. They partook of the wine Suggs found in a small bladder flask in his saddlebags, then saddled their horses and headed up into the rocky, deep-gullied, pine-studded foothills of the Black Widow Mountains. Raquella led the way, following an old prospector's trail she'd become familiar with when her family was hunting for their El Dorado up here.

The sun was bright, and the air was dry and cool, though thunderheads rumbled around to the north. Jackrabbits and deer abounded on the grassy slopes, and javelinas squealed in brambles and greasewood thickets. The higher they climbed, the cooler the air became, and by three o'clock they were all donning the serapes that had been tied around their bedrolls, and their breath puffed in the juniper-scented air.

Late in the day, when they were traversing a mesquite-tufted valley between pine-studded slopes, Longarm pulled back on his grulla's reins and held up his left hand for the others to do likewise. They were all familiar enough with the dangers of this Yaqui-infested country to hold their silence, but it wasn't an Indian that Longarm indicated on the shelf of brushy ground above them and right. It was a large, Sonoran buck with five points on one side of its enormous rack, six on the other. The big animal had its head down and hadn't yet caught the scent of the three riders.

Longarm lifted the barrel of the Winchester lying across his saddle bows. They were out of meat, and they might not get another chance at game before they were in the thick of Yaqui country. Slowly, making no sounds or sudden movement, the lawman stuck his reins in his teeth and placed his right hand on the rifle's cocking lever, ready to rack a fresh shell in the chamber.

Suddenly, the deer's black tail twitched and it raised its head sharply. There was a loud whump, and the big, dun body jerked as if from a massive muscle spasm. It shuffled sideways as the boom of a heavy-caliber rifle caromed out over the valley. The deer lifted its right rear hoof, but before it could set it down, it fell on its left side, quivered for a few seconds, legs twitching, and lay still.

Blood shone on its right shoulder. A heart shot.

Longarm slid his gaze up the ridge, but from this angle he couldn't see much farther up than where the buck had been grazing. He motioned to Suggs and Raquella and, without saying a word, they all reined their horses around and trotted back the way they'd come. They tied their horses in a clump of sprawling junipers, then, all holding rifles, scrambled up the ridge through stunted pines and aspens.

A couple minutes after leaving the horses, they hunkered in a grassy depression about thirty yards from where Longarm judged the buck had fallen. Longarm doffed his hat and edged a look over the depression's lip, staring down at the dead buck.

Looking right, he saw a young man walking a stout mule down from the rocky ridge crest, heading toward the buck. The younker wore a hooded coat of wolf fur, fringed deerskin breeches, and boot moccasins made from the same wolf as the coat. The hair falling forward from the hood was long, thick, and black.

In his left hand he carried a Spencer .56. The mule wore only a rawhide halter and a saddle blanket, with two large, canvas packs hanging down both sides of its belly. Another, smaller pouch was looped around the mule's neck, and several different kinds of roots protruded from the neck.

Longarm glanced at Suggs. They both looked around for more hunters. Spying no one, they glanced at each other again.

"Not dark enough for a Yaqui," Longarm muttered.

"Probably goat herder or some such," said Suggs.

To Longarm's right, Raquella stared at the young man and the mule with ridged brows.

Longarm laid his rifle in the grass and stood slowly. "Maybe we can buy a roast for tonight. The lad might know if there's Yaqui in the area too. You two stay down in case he's touchy."

He stepped onto the lip of the depression and raised his hand chest-high, palms out. *"Hola."*

The young man, ten feet from the buck now, whipped his head around and up so quickly that his hood fell back from his face. As he dropped the mule's lead rope and raised his Spencer to his shoulder, Longarm said in Spanish, "I mean you no harm! My friends and I were just passing through—"

Raquella's incredulous voice cut him off. "Rosa?"

The young stranger turned to Raquella kneeling behind the depression's lip, and Longarm saw the round, feminine face framed by the hood. A girl. Staring at Raquella, she blinked, and her eyes widened. *"Raquella?"*

Raquella stood, lower jaw hanging. "Ay! Sweet Mary in heaven—it is my lost sister!"

"Raquella!" Rosa laid her rifle down, and ran up the grade as Raquella ran down, flinging her arms out to her sides, her hat blowing off her head to hang down her back by the chin strap.

Raquella and Rosa met halfway between the two men and the mule, and threw their arms around each other. Raquella swung her sister in a circle, both girls' black hair flying out from their shoulders. Rosa was an inch or two shorter than Raquella, her face rounder and fuller, but even under the wolf coat, Longarm could tell she was put together as well as her sister.

The two girls kissed and hugged, conversing in hushed tones, tears rolling down their tan cheeks.

Longarm glanced at Suggs. "Small world."

The old scout shook his head and stared at the girls. "I figured she was dead."

"Señor Long! Señor Suggs!" Raquella said, throwing one arm around her sister's neck and facing both men with a broad, toothy smile, tears shining in her eyes. "I want you to meet the sister whom I thought I would never see again—Allysisa Rosa Concepción. Rosa, meet Señor Long and Señor Suggs. They are friends of mine. Without them, I never would have braved these mountains to find you!"

Rosa was considerably shier than her sister. She dropped her chin demurely, gave a little curtsy, and said in Spanish that she was honored to make their acquaintance.

"The pleasure's all ours," said Longarm in his best Spanish—which apparently wasn't very good, judging by Rosa's blush as she cut her eyes at her sister. "What are you doin' out here, miss? You are all alone?"

Raquella laughed at his goat-pen Spanish and answered for her sister, keeping her arm around Rosa's neck and giving the girl occasional, passionate kisses on her plump cheek. "Rosa escaped the Yaqui with the help of a padre from La Escondida. He took her under his wing, and they are traveling to the campesinos and shepherds too old or sick to travel to the church in the pueblo. They are camped on the mesa behind us. Rosa shot the deer for her and the padre's dinner."

Raquella rattled off some Spanish to her sister, then turned to Longarm and Suggs. "And Rosa has invited us to join them. The padre, she said, welcomes all strangers." She chuckled and threw her head back as she slanted a glance at her sister. "Even gringo strangers!"

"That's right kind of you, Miss Rosa," said Suggs, walking toward the dead deer while reaching for the broad-bladed knife on his left hip. "Me and Custis'll have this deer dressed out in just—"

He stopped as Rosa said something in Spanish that Longarm couldn't make out. As Rosa walked over and knelt beside the deer, drawing her own skinning knife from a sheath thonged on her thigh, Raquella said to Longarm and Suggs, "Rosa and I will dress the deer. She says that only she knows how to cut the meat the way the padre likes it."

As Raquella turned and strode over to the deer, drawing

her own stiletto, Suggs turned to Longarm and shrugged. "Well, hell, I never been against sitting around and watching women work!"

He set his rifle down and sat on the lip of the depression with a weary sigh, extending both buckskin-clad legs before him, heels in, bending his knees slightly.

Longarm glanced at the girls, prattling in Spanish as they set to work on the deer, working with practiced confidence.

"Me neither," he said, sitting down beside Suggs and plucking a cigar from his pocket.

When the girls had the deer dressed out, the organs and intestines carefully tied with rawhide and stowed in canvas sacks, Raquella ordered Longarm and Suggs to load the eviscerated carcass over the mule. Longarm and the old scout obeyed, then retrieved the horses for themselves and Raquella.

The sun was setting behind the Black Widows' highest western ridges when the group started up the grassy ridge, Raquella riding her horse while Rosa straddled the mule, in front of the gutted buck hanging limply down both sides of the mule's heavy flanks. The girls rode side by side, talking quietly, aware of the country's inherent dangers, while the men rode behind them.

The group rode up and over the ridge, across the narrow valley on the other side, then up the side of a sloping mesa wall, through boulders and gray-green sage and catclaw. Ahead, a vast, sandstone rimrock, blood-red with the plunging sun, rose like the hull of a giant Spanish galleon. The rimrock was probably a mile away, though in the clear mountain air it appeared close enough to touch.

Set against it, a small house of white rock stood amidst the sage at the crest of the gently sloping mesa. To one side, two paint horses grazed. Before the house, a small cook fire glowed, scenting the air with piñon.

146

"Maybe we oughta call out," Longarm said as the rock house grew before them, within fifty yards and closing. "Don't wanna scare the padre and draw a bullet."

"It would do little good," Raquella said, glancing over her shoulder at Longarm. "The padre is hard of hearing."

"Hope he's hard of shootin' then too," Suggs growled.

As Longarm followed the girls up to the rock house, he spied a tall, blocky figure in a dark-brown robe flanking the house on the right. The man had his back to the group, and he was looking down—apparently just standing there. One of the paints turned to the newcomers and whinnied loudly.

"Madre Mía!" the man in the sage exclaimed, wheeling around—a portly hombre with long, brown hair and a shaggy, salt-and-pepper beard. His robe was open, and he held one hand down by his crotch from which a thin stream trickled. He must have tripped on a log or a rock, because he gave another yell and, throwing his thick arms wide, dropped out of sight amongst the sage and creosote.

"Padre!" Rosa cried.

She was off the mule in a heartbeat and sprinting off through the sage, holding her rifle in her right hand. Longarm, Suggs, and Raquella heeled their horses ahead, weaving through the brush.

They drew rein as Rosa's head appeared from behind a clump of greasewood. The padre's head appeared then too—his broad face flushed, a chagrined smile lifting his beard. He straightened as Rosa held his arm and helped him draw his heavy, brown robe closed, then tie the rope around his portly waist. He chuckled and muttered in Spanish to Rosa, who prattled back at him, half-cajoling.

She led the padre toward Longarm, Suggs, and Raquella sitting their horses nearby. The padre approached Raquella's horse and said in surprisingly good English, "Ah, your sister, uh? What a wonderful surprise! I am Padre Baretto. Your sister has told me much about you, Raquella!"

"The pleasure is mine, Padre," Raquella said, shaking the padre's extended hand. "Thank you most kindly for taking such good care of my sister."

"Ah, it was a pleasure to free her from those savages." He glanced at Raquella's sister standing behind him, flushing. "Now, however, I fear I have grown too dependent on the girl. I no longer hunt for myself, as Rosa is a far better shot than I ever was. I no longer cook or pick up after myself. Hell, I can no longer even take a piss without wetting myself!"

The padre turned to Longarm and Suggs and threw his head back on his shoulders as deep laughter rumbled up from his belly. "What a sad state this old man has fallen into, eh, amigos?"

"Padre," Raquella said, indicating the two gringos beside her with an outstretched hand, "I would like to introduce my friends, Señor Long and Señor Suggs."

Longarm dismounted and shook hands with the padre, whose pudgy hand was soft though his grip was firm and energetic. "Pleased to meet you both, Señores. You will camp tonight with Rosa and me?"

"I never turn down a meal," Longarm said.

"And I doubt I ever will," Suggs added. "Custis and me'll un-mule that deer if'n you tell us where to put it."

When the men had hung the carcass head-down from a stout elm behind the ruined shack, the girls went to work bleeding it and carving roasts out of the cavity while Longarm and Suggs tended the horses and Rosa's mule, staking all four mounts out with the padre's two paints, who eyed the newcomers suspiciously, the white and brown one trotting around with its tail up.

It was good dark, stars wheeling overhead and coyotes yammering from the distant ridges, when they all sat around the fire, eating the roasted meet with warm tortillas, wild mint, and onions. Sage, currant shrubs, creosote, and rocks surrounded them, screening the fire from

148

all directions, and the smoke wafted straight up toward the stars.

After supper, the padre sank back against his saddle and asked Rosa to retrieve his bottle from his saddle pouch. When the girl had brought the demijohn, to which a horse-hair lanyard was attached, the padre filled each of their cups with a dry red wine. He gave some to the girls as well, then capped the flask and sank once more against his saddle, staring languidly into the flames still boiling grease from the roasted venison.

It was not in Padre Baretto's nature to ask questions, so Longarm told him what they were doing in Mexico and, briefly, what all they'd been through. The padre had no idea what Gatling guns were, so Suggs explained.

"And the Yaqui attacked an *americano* train to acquire such weapons?" asked the padre when he'd taken another sip of wine from his coffee cup, shifting his skeptical gaze between Longarm and Suggs. "That is very curious."

"How so?" asked Suggs.

"I did not think there were any groups of Yaqui large enough to attack a train in the United States. Not in northern Méjico, and not anymore. When the *americano* gold company and *mejicano* government opened the mine in La Escondida, the *rurales* and *federales* did a clean sweep of the country. Many of the troublemaking Yaquis were killed, the larger bands dispersed. Those who did not wish to work in the mine, I am saying.

"As it is, close to seventy Yaqui now work for the mine company, digging the gold from the Mountain of Saint Anthony near La Escondida. Many of the Yaqui have converted to Catholicism and worship in my church. I usually know what is happening amongst their people, and I have heard of no group riding north to steal weapons from the American government."

"Well, they probably wouldn't advertise it," Longarm said, staring into his wine cup. "Besides, we have reliable eyewitnesses who claim they saw Yaquis. And since we have no one else to go after, I reckon we'll continue on to La Escondida, check it out."

The padre stared across the fire at Longarm. "Maybe the thieves were the *rurales* who imprisoned you, dressed up like Yaquis? The *rurales* are nothing more than *bandidos* these days, crazy desert wolves running wild."

"We thought about that, Padre," said Suggs, blowing out a long stream of cigarette smoke. "The *rurales* that captured us was a band of misfits. Drunks and whoremongers, if you'll pardon my French. I don't think *they* even know why they locked us up. There ain't no way they had the *cojones* to take down that Peach Train."

The padre opened his mouth to speak, but Longarm waved him off, frowning at Suggs, who reclined on one hip and shoulder to his left. "Wait a minute. What's this about a 'Peach Train'?"

Suggs shrugged. "That's what the soldiers guarding the train hauling the Gatlings called it. On account o' someone having the bright idea of stamping 'peaches' on the crates those Gatlings was bein' shipped in." He chuckled. "Like that was gonna throw anybody off."

Longarm stared at him. His heart was beating fast. In his mind flashed the image of the three crates upon which the two *rurale* guards had been arm wrestling. He pushed himself up off the ground suddenly, and threw his cigar into the fire. "Well, it sure as shit threw us off!"

The padre frowned up at him. The girls, who'd been talking quietly at one end of the fire, with Rosa resting her head atop Raquella's belly, fell suddenly silent as they too stared up at the lawman.

"Calm down, Custis," Suggs said cautiously. "I do believe you're getting' desert crazy."

"Those long crates the *rurales* in the jail block were using for a table had 'peaches' stamped on their sides." Longarm stared hard at Suggs. "Didn't you see?"

An indignant cast came to the scout's one good eye as he pushed off his shoulder. "Hell, Custis, you know I can't *read*!" He rose to his knees and slapped his thighs. "You mean to tell me we was practically sittin' *right on top of those Gatlin' guns*?"

Chapter 17

"Those damn *rurales* attacked that train after all," Longarm said, sitting down on a log and staring incredulously at the fire. "How did they do it? More importantly, *why* did they do it? Why do they want those guns?"

"I could see if they were having partic'lar bad trouble with the Yaqui," Suggs said, leaning forward to accept another dollop of wine from the padre. "But the padre said the Yaqui been held at bay." Suggs glanced at the man as he tipped more wine into Longarm's cup. "You have any idea what they intend to hit, Father?"

Baretto straightened and capped the demijohn. He swayed a little on his feet. The wine had some teeth to it. "The only thing worth robbing in this part of Chihuahua would be the gold mine at La Escondida. But it is heavily guarded by *federales*."

"You say the mine is co-owned by an American company," Longarm said. "Assuming they ship some of the gold to the border, you know how they do it?"

"By train. When the mine was opened, a spur track was laid between La Escondida and the main line at Río Ojo." The padre's jaw dropped as he stared into the darkness beyond the fire. *"Ay caramba!"*

Longarm glanced at Suggs, then turned back to the padre. "What is it, Father?"

"What day is it?"

Longarm thought for a moment. "Thursday."

"Mierda," whispered the padre. "The lieutenant of the mine told me they intended to ship the gold on Friday. Their largest load so far!"

Suggs looked at Longarm. "That would explain why Santangelo didn't bother giving us chase. He was more worried about stopping that train."

"It ain't hard to stop a train," Longarm said. "And with those three Gatling guns placed high above the tracks, they could mow down the guards—even if the guards have their own Gatlings—like ducks on a millpond."

Longarm turned to the padre, still standing by the fire, swaying slightly on his moccasin-clad feet. "Any idea what time the train pulls out of La Escondida?"

Baretto shook his head. "I know not, Señor."

"Even if we knew the timetable," Suggs said, doffing his hat with frustration and scratching his head, "how in tarnation we gonna find the spot on the tracks the *rurales* intend to hit?"

"I rode the train once." The padre walked slowly around the fire and sat down heavily by his saddle, quilts, and blankets. He looked across the fire at Longarm and Suggs, the flames flickering in his rheumy brown eyes. "They always stop for water at Arroyo de los Santos. It was once a *pueblecito,* but a sickness and Yaqui attacks took their toll on the inhabitants. There is now only a railroad shack and a water tank running through the shallow canyon. It is the first stop on the line. The rest of the route, until they reach the plains near Río Ojo, is through deep, narrow chasms, the bottoms of which would be nearly impossible to reach with horses."

Suggs squinted his good eye at Longarm. "There we have it."

Longarm stared at the priest. "How far from here is Arroyo de los Santos?"

The padre shrugged and lifted his left arm to point behind him. "You are practically there, Señores. It is just beyond that big mesa. A two-hour ride at the most."

Longarm glanced over his wine cup at Suggs. "We'll get started first thing in the morning. I reckon we just have to hope we get there before the train does."

"But you are only two men," Raquella put in. She was sitting on her heels now, back taut, hands on her thighs. "How could you stop *rurales*—twenty, maybe thirty men—armed with such powerful guns?"

Suggs turned to Longarm with a bitter expression. Longarm mirrored it.

"That's one we're gonna have to sleep on," Longarm said, and threw back the last of his wine.

Since most of the Yaqui in this part of the country had been tamed for the moment, Longarm and Suggs saw no reason to keep a night watch. But when Longarm had tossed and turned in his blankets for nearly a half hour, his mind too busy for sleep, he grabbed his Winchester and walked away from the figures reclining around the low fire, into the crisp, cool night.

His breath puffed before him. The crunch of his boots in the fine gravel and dry, brown grass sounded like muffled pistol fire in the dense, high-country silence.

When he was a good fifty yards from the camp, he sat on a large boulder and stared at the hull-like ridge rising in the northeast, silhouetted against the frosty stars, and fired his last cheroot. Staring at the black ridge, cupping the cigar in the palm of his right hand, he yearned for the dawn to show itself behind the eastern mountains so he and Suggs could saddle up and head for Arroyo de los Santos.

Santangelo was probably having himself a good laugh, having made fools of the two gringos by jailing them both within thirty feet of the crated Gatling guns. A real good laugh. Longarm couldn't wait to wipe the smile off the *rurale*'s face.

Soft footfalls sounded behind him. As he turned his head to one side, Raquella said softly, "It's me."

He turned forward, heard her footsteps grow louder until he could feel the warmth of her body beside him.

He took another drag off his cheroot. "You couldn't sleep either?"

She snugged her head against his shoulder. "I was *cold*." She took his hand in hers and stepped out ahead of him. "Rosa told me of a *warm* place."

He frowned at her standing before him, a blanket around her shoulders, her legs naked, moccasins on her feet. Her full breasts pushed at the blanket. She pulled on his arm. "Come."

He slid off the boulder. "Where we goin'?"

"I will show you." She slid her eyes coyly away as she began leading him off through the sage, in the direction of the large ridge hulking before them.

Resting the Winchester on his right shoulder, Longarm followed Raquella across the mesa and down the other side, the girl pulling him along through the brush, zigzagging around weed-choked boulders and dwarf cedars. The smell of sulfur spiced the air, growing stronger the farther they angled down the mesa's gentle slope, a steam cloud rising before them, gauzy-gray in the darkness.

As they rounded a jumble of black boulders, the air warmed. There was the sound of water trickling over rocks. They pushed through the brush, and a tar-black pool opened before them, bathed in fog and surrounded by mounds of black lava rock and lush grass.

"Look!" Raquella said, releasing Longarm's hand and kneeling beside the pool. She dipped a hand into the water. "A hot bath!"

156

She stood, threw her arms around him, and kissed him. Then she stepped straight back, tossed her blanket onto a boulder, and lifted her poncho up and over her head. She wore nothing under it. As she tossed it onto the boulder with the blanket, her hair spilled across her naked shoulders, thick strands snaking across her breasts, which were full and deep and pushing proudly out from her chest.

Longarm lowered his rifle and reached for her, but she wheeled away with a laugh, sat down at the edge of the pool, and dropped her long legs into the water. Longarm's pulse throbbed in his throat as she lowered herself into the pool, sighing and groaning and cupping the steaming water up her arms and over her chest. Her back was slender, flaring at her hips, and her breasts shone like half-moons under her arms.

"The water is wonderful!" she said, moving to the other side of the pool and turning to him, the water coming up to just above her belly.

While she continued luxuriating in the warmth, Longarm set his rifle on a boulder, kicked out of his boots, and was out of his clothes in under a minute. His shaft jutting before him, he stepped to the edge of the pool. At the other side, she watched him silently as she slowly cupped water over her breasts.

He hoisted himself into the water, which was a degree or so cooler than a hot bath, the warm steam smelling like hot iron. The uneven bottom was pebbled, with occasional sharp rocks.

Longarm made his way quickly across the pool, took Raquella in his arms, tipped her head back on her shoulders, and stared down at her. His jutting member pressed against the warm, wet mat between her thighs.

She stared back at him, her full lips parted. "I have never belonged to any man, but tonight I am yours!"

He closed his mouth over hers and kissed her for a long time, enjoying the feel of her lips against his, their tongues entangling. His member grew even harder and more demanding and, as if of its own accord, found her hot portal and began to penetrate.

She gasped, and then their mouths came apart as, with an almost violent surge, he lifted her suddenly half out of the water. He placed his hands on the backs of her thighs and hoisted her up to his waist. Digging her fingers into his biceps, she entangled her legs around him as he turned his back toward the edge of the pool and lowered her slowly down on his shaft.

"Mierda!" She threw her head back and opened her mouth, digging her fingers farther into his arms and crossing her ankles behind his back.

Cradling her in her arms, his hands closed over the backs of her shoulders, he lifted her out to the end of his cock and then pulled her back down again.

"Dios mío!" she cried as he repeated the maneuver, then held her suspended there at the end of his shaft, savoring the sweet misery.

She begged him to impale her again, grinding her heels into his back. He waited a couple of counts, slid her down hard, lifted her away, then pulled her down again.

Her head bobbed, her hair spilled into the water, and her breasts bounced as he shoved her out and then brought her back in, ramming his cock deep into her hot chasm again and again with such fury that the water splashed over the side of the pool to slide like oil across the rocks.

When he felt her core contracting and spasming, he thrust her away from him, intending to delay the end.

"No, you crazy gringo!" she fairly screamed, grabbing his shoulders and pulling him back into her. *"Finish me!"*

He brought her back in and finished her.

Still jerking against him, she leaned forward, placed her hand on his cheek, and kissed him, sliding her tongue down his throat. Pulling it back out, she bit his lower lip, sighed deeply, and let her head sag against his shoulder.

158

He drew a deep breath as the steaming water and the lovemaking conspired to make his limbs and eyelids heavy. He lifted his gaze above the far side of the pool, and felt as though he'd been braced with a bucket of snowmelt.

Obscured by the webbing steam tendrils, Lee Suggs stood at the far side of the pool, dressed in only his long underwear, hat, and boots, his rifle in his hands. Beside him stood Padre Baretto in his brown robe, his long, gray hair mussed from sleep. He held a pistol in his hand. Rosa stood beside the padre, her black hair hanging to her shoulders. The young girl stared down at Longarm and Raquella, holding a hand to her flushed right cheek, her chest rising and falling sharply.

"Jesus Christ, Custis," Suggs growled as he scowled down at the two lovers in the pool. "Don't you know how sound carries in the high country?"

Raquella yowled and jerked a startled glance over her shoulder. Suggs chuckled and walked away while the padre grinned sheepishly.

"I apologize for the intrusion," he said, bowing his shaggy, leonine head. "But we thought someone was being murdered out here."

When he'd shuffled off behind Suggs, Rosa stepped toward the pool, balling her shirttails in her fists and regarding her sister with gravity. She and Raquella exchanged a few words in rapid Spanish, and the younger sister bunched her lips with disappointment, lowered her chin, and strode away.

Longarm looked at Raquella, her face only inches from his. "What'd she say?"

"She asked if she could have a go with the handsome gringo who must be much man to make a woman scream with such abandon." Raquella curled her upper lip. "I told her she was too young for such a man"—she swiped a lock of damp hair from his eyes—"that you were *almost* too much man for me."

She leaned toward him, took his head in his hands, and kissed him.

After a time, he pulled away with a weary sigh. "We best get back to the camp." He grinned. "After all that, I have a feelin' I'm gonna sleep just fine."

"I will make sure."

She wriggled out of his grasp, dropped her feet to the bottom of the pool, then kissed her way down his broad chest and flat belly until her head disappeared beneath the swirling black water.

He closed his eyes, tipped his head back, and groaned.

Chapter 18

After making love with Raquella in the hot water, Longarm slept as well as he thought he would. Too well, in fact. Suggs had to wake him with a kick to his backside.

In the false dawn's purple shadows, both men dressed in silence, so as not to waken Raquella, Rosa, and the padre, who all continued slumbering around the fire's cold ashes. The men gathered their gear, made sure their weapons were loaded, then headed into the brush to saddle their horses.

Longarm was strapping his rifle boot to the right side of his saddle when he heard footsteps and turned to see Raquella, silhouetted against the lightening sky, moving toward him through the brush. Fully dressed, her man's hat thonged beneath her chin, she carried her saddle on her right shoulder.

Longarm glanced at Suggs, who was tying his bedroll behind his cantle, then turned back to the girl. "What do you think you're doing?"

"I am coming with you."

As she headed for her horse, Longarm stepped in front of her. "No, you're not. You're staying here with the padre and your sister."

161

She looked up at him, her eyes sparking. "Two men have no chance against the *rurales* and their Gatling guns. You will need help. At the very least you will need someone to distract them while you locate the guns."

"Forget it. It's too dangerous and it ain't your fight. You ain't even getting paid."

Softly, moisture glistening in her eyes, she said, "You have no chance."

"I work better that way."

He glanced at Suggs, who stared at him and the girl over his horse's rump. Longarm took Raquella's arm and led her several yards back toward the camp. When they were out of the old scout's field of vision, Longarm grabbed her and kissed her, knocking her hat down her back. He pulled away and gazed down at her, swept her hair back from her shoulder, and caressed her cheek with the back of his hand.

Gently, he said, "Stay here. If we're not back in twenty-four hours, hightail it with the padre and your sister to La Escondida."

He started back toward the horses.

"You cannot keep me from following you."

He stopped, turned toward her once more, and squinted his right eye. "No, but I *can* run you down and tie your pretty ass to a tree."

With that, he continued to the horses and resumed strapping his rifle boot to his saddle. Behind him, Suggs chuckled as he heaved himself onto his buckskin. "You ever go anywhere without gettin' yourself mired in female trouble?"

Longarm moved around his horse and swung into the saddle. "What would life be without female trouble, Lee?"

They mounted up and put their horses in the direction the padre had drawn out for them in the dirt the night before. They rode out across the mesa and followed a game trail down the other side and into an arroyo in the valley below.

By sunrise, they were skirting the south side of the ship-like mountain, the morning light pointing up the striations in the wall and showing the pictographs painted there a thousand years ago.

They meandered through a canyon so narrow that light probably found it for only a few minutes each day. A half hour later, they rode up out of the canyon to a boulder-strewn ridge, amongst which were scattered the old, sun-bleached bones of some unfortunate human wayfarer, and checked down their horses.

Dismounting, Longarm fished a spyglass from the saddlebags, and followed Suggs to a wedge between two boulders at the very top of the bluff. Hugging the rock's cool, concealing shadows, Longarm brushed the lens across his sleeve, then raised it to his right eye, slowly adjusting the focus until a wide arroyo swam into focus below.

Bordered on the far side by a rocky, sandstone slope, the canyon was cleaved by a freshly graded rail bed mounded with white gravel and capped by glistening iron rails. On the right side of the tracks lay the scattered ruins of an ancient town—crumbling rock foundations and disintegrating stone and adobe hovels surrounding a church that stood only about thirty yards from the rail bed.

The church was sun-bleached and cracked, with half its rear wall lying in the sage and gravel, exposing the church's core. Most of the roof's red tiles were missing, but the bell tower remained, like the empty eye socket of a decayed skull.

Only, the tower wasn't empty. As Longarm adjusted the spyglass's focus, he could see men moving around inside. Sunlight winked off the brass housing of what was most likely one of the three Gatling guns.

He moved the spyglass down. Several horses and *rurales* milled around behind the church and the other ruins. Four squatted around a low coffee fire in the shade of a spindly mesquite. One sat on a crumbling wall, cleaning the rifle resting across his thighs.

They all kept the ruins between them and the railroad tracks.

"Our boys are here," Longarm said, lowering the spyglass to peer with his naked eyes down the slope. "But I've found only one gun."

"Look over there," Suggs said, pointing toward the low, salmon-colored ridge on the east side of the tracks.

Longarm raised the glass to his right eye, again adjusted the focus. He swept the slope, letting the glass linger first on one brass barrel jutting from a rock nest directly across from the church and about sixty yards above the tracks, then on another snub-nosed Gatling hunkered in the shade beneath a house-sized wedge of exposed andosite. He couldn't see how many men were manning the first gun, but two sombrero-capped silhouettes flanked the second, one *rurale* bringing a cigarette to his lips and gesturing with one hand to his compadre.

Longarm stretched his lips back from his teeth. "I've got the other two Gatlings." He offered the glass to Suggs. "Wanna look?"

"Hell, no," the old scout said proudly, squinting his lone good eye toward the ridge. "I can see both those brass canisters fine. What I wanna know is . . . how you wanna play this?"

Longarm glassed the ridge again, then the ruined town and church and the shadows moving in the bell tower.

"Too many in the town," he said. "Getting into the bell tower—too risky. I say we take out the *rurales* on the left end of the ridge with our knives and, if we don't have time to slip over and take out the second, take out the other two Gatlings with the first."

Suggs was grinning at him.

"What?" Longarm said.

"I love your sand, Custis. Hell, I think you think we can actually *pull* this off—two men against twenty in full daylight."

Longarm reduced the spyglass and headed back around the boulder toward the horses. "I only counted seventeen."

When Longarm and Suggs had secured their horses in a wide patch of shade at the rear base of the ridge, loosened their saddle cinches, and slipped the bits from their mouths, they grabbed their rifles and headed on foot through a deep gully straight north from the ruined village and the *rurale* encampment. They found an intersecting arroyo lined with brush, and followed the cut straight east, pausing to peer over the arroyo's lip every few minutes so they didn't lose the salmon ridge they were heading for.

They moved quickly, sweating and breathing hard.

Since the *rurales* had assumed positions around the guns, the train would likely be pulling through soon, right into a storm of .45-caliber lead spat like hail from the devil's mouth, if Longarm and Suggs didn't emasculate the Gatlings in time.

Fortunately, no train in Mexico ever ran on time.

When they were well behind the face of the ridge, they scrambled up out of the arroyo, jogged to the ridge's boulder-strewn base, and climbed the north shoulder. Fifteen feet from the ridge, Longarm leaped a boulder. To his right a hiss sounded, like a taut lariat raked against a tree, and there was a gray flash of movement from behind a Spanish bayonet plant.

The snake smashed its open mouth and exposed fangs against his boot heel as Longarm sucked a startled breath and lit on the flat rock above. "Watch it, Lee."

Suggs stood on a boulder ten feet behind him, his Spencer in both hands as he eyed the snake warily. The Mojave green rattler lay coiled tightly, its rattle-studded tail and diamond-shaped head raised with threat.

Suggs looked around. The boulders on both sides of his path were too high to climb easily. With his right hand, he extended his rifle toward the snake. As the viper struck, the scout snagged its neck by the barrel and flicked it off down the slope, where it landed with a thud, the rattling growing louder, more furious.

As Suggs took two long strides toward Longarm, he said, keeping his voice low, "You know how I know the Lord hates men?"

"Because of snakes?"

"And thick-ankled women."

"Come on."

They gained the ridge, studied the slope before them. It dropped at about a forty-five-degree angle into a nest of rocks, which Longarm recognized as the one where the *rurales* had secured the first Gatling. He couldn't see the gun or the *rurales* from this angle, but he'd marked the spot by a cedar growing nearly sideways from a cracked boulder.

Beneath the gun nest, the slope dropped for another two hundred feet to the arroyo floor. Beyond lay the glistening iron rails and the bleached white church and the ruined hovels around which nearly a dozen *rurales* stood, casting frequent glances south along the rail bed.

Hunkered behind a scarp, Longarm glanced at Suggs, who voiced the question on the lawman's mind. "How in hell we gonna work our way down to that nest without getting spotted from across the arroyo?"

Longarm cursed and studied the slope, then cast his glance once more across the arroyo. He turned to Suggs. "I think they're all too busy watchin' for the train. Let's go, *and stay low!*"

Longarm slipped out from behind the scarp and ran down the incline, crouching and zigzagging between brush clumps and boulders. Behind him, Suggs cursed and grumbled, "A man my age can get only so low before he can't get *up* again!"

Longarm kept an eye peeled on the *rurales* as he dropped down the slope, pausing occasionally to crouch behind a shrub or a rock. When he was within twenty feet of the gun nest, he slowed down so his footsteps wouldn't be heard by the *rurales* manning the Gatling.

When he was within ten feet of the nest, one of the *rurales* milling along the railroad bed—Santangelo, judging by the man's short, heavy-gutted frame and leather-billed officer's cap—turned to stare up the ridge.

Longarm dropped to his knees and pressed his right shoulder hard against a boulder, waving for Suggs to hunker low as well.

When Suggs had thrown himself between two low rocks, kicking gravel down the slope before him, Longarm doffed his hat and edged a look around his covering boulder. Desultory Spanish rose from the rock nest below and left. Across the arroyo, Santangelo continued staring in Longarm's direction, one high-topped black boot propped on a rail.

The lawman gritted his teeth. It looked as though the *rurale* major was staring right at him, maybe trying to figure out what had caused that shadow to flicker along the ridge. Trying to decide whether to send men over or shout a warning to those hunkering down around the Gatling gun.

"Goddamnit," Longarm grated softly through gritted teeth, his heart tattooing his breast bone. "Turn away, you fat . . ."

As though obeying Longarm's command, Santangelo turned his head slowly to scrutinize the other end of the ridge. A few seconds later, his head continued swiveling until the bill of his hat faced south.

Longarm glanced at Suggs, who gave his head a relieved shake. Then the lawman continued moving down the slope and left, stopping when he smelled cigarette smoke. He looked through the giant boulders on his right.

Through a two-foot crack, he saw a middle-aged *rurale* standing before the Gatling gun, which, mounted on a tripod and with its crank handle raised and ready, stood about five feet off the ground. Its barrel was aimed between two more boulders and slanted down the slope toward the rails. The *rurale* stood sideways, talking to someone on his left, a thin, black cigar smoldering in his left hand.

Longarm gestured for Suggs to steal around the rocks and take the unseen *rurale* from the left. When the scout leaned his rifle against the boulder, shucked his bowie knife, and stole quietly away, Longarm set his own rifle down and unsheathed one of the stilettos he'd found amongst the stolen *bandido* gear.

He waited for five seconds, giving Suggs time to get set, then slipped sideways through the slot. The *rurale* stopped talking instantly and wheeled toward him, eyes widening and lower jaw dropping.

Longarm lunged forward, bringing up the stiletto underhanded and driving the razor-sharp blade into the man's belly. It ticked off a brass button, then angled straight up under the man's rib cage and into his heart.

Longarm released the handle as the man groaned and doubled up, liver-colored blood and intestines spewing from the wound. He stepped back as the *rurale* dropped to his knees, wheezing, eyelids fluttering. To his left, the other *rurale* stared at Longarm, his eyes glazing in death as Suggs pushed him down with one gloved hand atop the private's right shoulder.

The private's knees buckled, and he fell straight down and forward, piling up at Longarm's boots with a loud fart. Above and behind him, Suggs stood holding the blood-washed bowie in his right fist.

Longarm kicked over the *rurale* he'd killed, reached for the stiletto still lodged in the dead man's gut, and stopped suddenly. A voice rose from behind Suggs, who stepped quickly behind a boulder and held the bowie up high against his chest. Longarm stepped behind a curve in the boulder on his left.

"*Chavez! Ortega!*" someone shouted, boots loudly grinding gravel near the boulder snag. He told them in

Spanish little better than Longarm's that the train's smoke had been seen on a distant incline, and ordered the two *rurales* to get into firing position.

The man's voice struck Longarm as familiar, and he edged a look around the boulder's curve. He blinked as if to clear his vision. The man striding toward him, while not clad in U.S. Army blues but in black jeans, blue-plaid shirt, cowhide vest, and cream Stetson, was Major Artemis St. George, chief commanding officer of Fort Sabre.

Longarm glanced at Suggs. The scout had angled his own glance around the boulder behind him, and he returned Longarm's incredulous stare.

The boots stopped on the gravel, and St. George grunted fiercely. Longarm glanced at St. George, who stood just outside the boulder nest, leaning forward slightly, his right hand on the New Line .41 holstered on his right hip, his keen blue eyes riveted on Longarm.

"What the *fuck*?" St. George raked out.

Longarm grinned savagely. "I reckon I know why we were after Yaquis instead of *rurales,* you son of a bitch."

He had no choice. As St. George began to slip his own revolver from its sheath, Longarm slapped leather, aimed his Colt, and fired.

The revolver's crack echoed like thunder around the canyon.

Chapter 19

Longarm's bullet took St. George through the forehead. The major gave a sharp grunt as he twisted back and fell facedown amongst the rocks and cactus.

"Shit!" Suggs said.

Longarm leaped forward and edged a look around one of the boulders forming the nest. On the arroyo below, Santangelo had turned back to the ridge and was casting his gaze toward the nest, shading his eyes with a hand held above his hat brim. The dozen or so *rurales* flanking him were turning toward the ridge as well, a couple stooping to pick up their rifles, which had been resting against the train rails.

Longarm raised his gaze to the church's bell tower, where two flat brown faces stared out on either side of the protruding muzzle of the Gatling gun. As Santangelo turned toward the bell tower, Suggs said, "Hold your hat, Custis, I'm gonna unleash the hounds of war!"

On the other side of the boulders to Longarm's right, the Gatling began roaring—a guttural rattle that made the rocks and the ground beneath the lawman's boots vibrate. Down on the arroyo, the forty-five-caliber slugs blew up chunks of dust and gravel, a few sparking off the train rails as a couple of the *rurales* screamed and fell, the rest scattering and charging for cover.

Several slugs chewed up the ground behind Santangelo, tracking the *rurale* major as he bolted down the railroad grade so quickly that he lost his hat and dove behind the ruined stone wall of a goat pen.

Longarm laughed as he retrieved his Winchester, hearing the rataplan of the Gatling gun and the screech of ricocheting bullets below the ridge. "Give 'em hell, Lee!" Back on the south side of the rock nest, he raised the rifle to his shoulder and began adding his own barrage to that of the Gatling.

Suggs was now concentrating his fire on the bell tower, the Gatling's slugs chewing up the adobe around the opening from which the muzzle protruded. The men had ducked out of sight, no doubt befuddled by the sudden attack. Several shots sparked off the barrel with sharp clangs. Below, Santangelo was shouting orders behind the ruined wall of the goat pen.

As the Gatling continued roaring, Longarm blew out the knee of a *rurale* attempting to gain the base of the ridge. As the man fell, Longarm fired again, but beneath the Gatling's staccato bellowing he heard only the ping of the Winchester's hammer hitting the firing pin without igniting a cartridge.

He pulled back behind the rock to thumb cartridges through the Winchester's loading gate. Doing so, he stared down the slope. A handful of *rurales* broke from cover and sprinted up and over the railroad grade, heading toward the ridge's base.

"They're moving on us, Lee!"

There was a pause in the Gatling's barrage before it started again, and two of the *rurales* crossing the rail bed dropped amidst a barrage of lead, grimacing and losing their rifles. Santangelo and several others continued to the ridge and dropped down behind rocks.

At the same time, several slugs plunked into the boulders fronting the nest, followed a half second later by the hiccups of the Gatling gun in the church's bell tower. Around the rotating canister, flames stabbed and smoke gushed.

Rock shards and dust blew up and over Longarm, a couple of slugs tearing into the brush beside him, a couple more plunking into St. George's corpse, jostling the body and spraying blood across the gravel. Longarm dove into the boulder nest as a bullet clipped his boot and tore through the slack of a trouser leg.

To his right, Suggs was hunkered down behind the Gatling gun as slugs barked off the gun's housing and pelted the rocks before him. Suggs winced and looked at Longarm.

"Fuckin' gun jammed. That's the problem with a Gatling gun. They get too fuckin' hot and they jam!"

"Remind me not to get you one for Christmas," Longarm said, heaving himself to his feet and peering around the left side of the rock nest.

Ten or so *rurales* were running up the ridge, spread out and howling like Apaches. Several were triggering lead as they ran. Behind them, hunkered behind a boulder at the base of the ridge, Santangelo shouted orders to kill the gringo bastards and to bring him their heads.

Longarm looked straight across the slope. A slight rise blocked his view of the other Gatling gun. He turned back to Suggs as bullets plunked around him.

"Let's make a run for the other gun!"

Suggs shook his head. He raised his Spencer in one hand. "I'll cover you from here."

Longarm bolted forward across the slope, digging his boot heels into the slanting, rocky turf as he made for a wagon-sized boulder up the slope ten yards and thirty yards across. Down the slope, the *rurales* yelled and slung lead at him.

Bullets buzzed like hornets, ricocheting, shattering cactus plants, and kicking up caliche and sage and juniper branches. Suggs went to work with the Spencer, and several *rurales* dove for cover. Longarm returned fire with the Winchester, crouching and levering shells and slanting the barrel across his belly.

Gaining the cover of the large boulder, he jacked another shell, took a breath, then bolted back out from behind the rock and laid out two *rurales* running toward him from thirty yards away. He turned and ran out from the other side of the boulder, continuing across the ridge slope toward the Gatling gun nested a hundred yards farther on.

Apparently realizing where he was headed, the *rurales* switched direction and were now running toward the other Gatling. It was a footrace, the *rurales* now running more than shooting, to see who could get behind the deadly Gatling first.

Behind Longarm, Suggs's firing had died.

Longarm misjudged a leap over a rock and fell, sending the Winchester skidding across the ground before him. He picked it up as he glanced right to see the *rurales* sprinting up the slope and angling toward the nest. A half-dozen others trailed, lips stretched back from their teeth as they sucked air into their lungs and continued scrambling through the rocks and prickly scrub brush.

Longarm had the fewest yards to cover—the nest was only forty yards away, in a natural barricade of domino-shaped rocks, cactus, and Spanish bayonet—but he had to take care of the men inside before he could man the gun.

A couple of the *rurales,* behind him and right, triggered a couple of shots. Twenty yards from the Gatling nest, he stopped, dropped to a knee, and fired three quick rounds in return, sending two *rurales* flying and delaying the others. He bounded off his heels and sprinted as fast as he could for the last few yards, and leaped onto a boulder. Aiming the Winchester from his right hip, he stared into the hollow below.

The Gatling stood on its tripod in the rocks to the right, barrel extending between two boulders. In the hollow to the left, Padre Baretto lay on his back, holding his right hand to his bloody left shoulder, his eyes rolling around in their sockets as though he were dazed. At his feet lay a dead *rurale,* belly down, a stiletto sticking out of his back. Nearby, another *rurale* lay facedown atop someone struggling beneath him. The *rurale* was cursing, both hands beneath his chest, his head bobbing from side to side as he wrestled, legs thrashing.

As the scattered *rurale* group approached from down the slope, stitching the air around Longarm's head with bullets, he snapped his Winchester to his shoulder and drew a bead on the *rurale* private struggling in the hollow. He flicked his finger from the trigger when a girl screamed viciously and a bare, tan leg whipped out from beneath the *rurale*'s right thigh.

The *rurale* cursed and then flopped over on his back. Raquella bounded off the ground and threw herself atop the *rurale,* screaming like a witch as she planted a pistol barrel against the underside of the *rurale*'s chin.

Pop!

The *rurale* had opened his mouth to scream, but the bullet slammed his mouth closed before careening out the top of his head in a spray of brain, bone, and blood. Raquella bobbed her head as she spat in the dead man's face, then jerked her head suddenly to Longarm, whipping the pistol out before her and clicking the hammer back. She lowered the pistol a wink later, and the lines in her forehead planed out.

Longarm leaped off the barricade wall and into the hollow, slugs spanging off the rocks around him.

"I thought I told you to stay put!"

"I got bored."

Longarm hunkered down behind the Gatling gun. Two *rurales* were within ten yards and closing fast, screaming like Apaches closing for the kill.

"Looks like your boredom bought the padre a bullet!" Longarm snapped, wincing as a blue whistler cleaved a crack in the rocks to rake a burn across his cheek.

He grabbed the crank handle, swung the Gatling canister right, and angled it down the slope. One of the two *rurales* stopped to raise his rifle. Longarm grimaced against the burn in his cheek and against another bullet whistling inches over his left shoulder, and swung the crank. As the Gatling's canister began rotating, opening up with its thunderous rat-a-tat of exploding .45 shells, loud as a stampeding herd of bull buffalo, the *rurale* who'd been aiming his rifle disappeared in a spray of red, flinging his rifle high and behind him.

A half second later, three more slugs tore across the chest of the *rurale* flanking the first, and Longarm continued swinging the canister right and left and back again, turning the crank and loosing a hail of lead through dove-gray uniform tunics, punching the howling *rurales* back down the hill and across the rocks and shrubs, screaming and clutching their heads and throats and bellies and thighs while blood splattered and guns flew.

When all the *rurales* appeared down, Longarm held fire and stared through the smoke. Silence. He'd begun to ease his grip on the crank's wooden handle when he spied movement to his left. He swung the canister as a *rurale* bolted up from behind a boulder and snugged his cheek against the stock of his extended Spencer carbine.

Longarm blasted the boulder and ground around it with about eight slugs, and the *rurale*'s face became a tomato before it disappeared behind the boulder.

Longarm held the crank handle and raked his gaze along the quiet slope, then angled it across the arroyo to the church, showing white in the late-morning sunlight. A body hung over the outside wall, just right of the Gatling's protruding muzzle, the man's arms dangling toward the ground. Below him, the adobe was streaked with red. No shadows moved in the opening above him.

"Who needs a fucking Gatlin'?"

It was Lee Suggs, moving along the slope to Longarm's right, holding his Spencer down low in his right hand. The scout's hat was gone. He was so dusty and bloody, his clothes so disheveled, that he could have just climbed out of a caved-in mine. A lock of curly, pewter hair hung down over his pearl-gray eye while the good one squinted with amusement.

Suggs held up his rifle. "Give me a trusty Spencer any old day."

Longarm looked around behind him. Raquella was sitting beside the padre, holding a bandanna inside the man's brown robe, over his shoulder.

The lawman stretched another gaze into the arroyo, then glanced at Suggs, who continued walking toward him over the rocks. Longarm cleared the cordite from his throat. "Where's Santangelo?"

Suggs stumbled on a stone. "I figured you got him."

As if to punctuate the sentence, the rattling concussion of a Gatling sounded. Suggs screamed as bullets plunked up dust around him, spanging and whining and tearing pieces from the rocks and boulders. Longarm ducked as two bullets sparked across the Gatling's canister and blew his hat off, punching him back off his haunches to hit the hollow on his back. Raquella screamed as several bullets raked the rocks inches above her and the padre's heads.

Longarm climbed back up behind the Gatling gun. Keeping his head down, he edged a look over the rocks to his right, where Suggs lay facedown and unmoving. In the church's bell tower, a bulky silhouette with an officer's billed cap shone over the Gatling's smoking barrel.

"Son of a bitch," Longarm growled as he tipped up the

barrel of his own Gatling, taking aim on the church and giving the crank a savage turn.

Phat-a-bat-bat-bat-bat-bat!

Slugs tore into and around the belfry's opening, blowing adobe chunks from the wall and ricocheting off the Gatling's barrel with ringing clanks. The cacophony had barely started before Santangelo's head ducked out of sight, but Longarm kept turning his Gatling's crank until he'd emptied the clip and the canister froze, smoke rising around the brass casing like fog off a stream.

Longarm grabbed his rifle and leaped over the barricade wall, running toward Suggs, who still lay unmoving in the rocks about thirty yards away.

"Look there!" Raquella called behind Longarm.

He glanced at her, then followed her pointing arm into the arroyo. A horse and rider were galloping north from the church, angling toward the arroyo. Santangelo was hunkered low in the saddle, urging the steeldust with his spurred boot heels.

Longarm raised his rifle in both hands, scrambled down the slope toward the arroyo. Stopping, he jacked a shell into the Winchester's chamber, knelt, and raised the butt to his shoulder.

Santangelo was a good hundred and fifty yards away and fleeing fast.

Longarm led Santangelo by a good ten feet, and squeezed the trigger. The slug drilled the ground with a dust puff, and horse and rider continued dwindling into the distance.

Longarm rammed another shell into the breech, lined up his sights on the major's back, then raised them a good two finger widths above the man's bobbing head. He held his breath, and let his finger take the slack out of the trigger.

Boom!

"Shit!" Longarm shouted as Santangelo continued fading into the brassy, dusty desert.

He was about to rise, then, continuing to stare after the horse and rider, froze. Santangelo sagged slightly to one side. The major caught himself, then continued sagging to his left until his left shoulder hit the ground.

His left boot got hung up in the stirrup, and the horse dragged the major, bobbing his head and back along the ground like a child's rubber ball, for a good fifty yards. The boot came loose and Santangelo slid several yards before rolling another ten and piling up against a nest of black rocks.

He was too far away for Longarm to see clearly, but Santangelo appeared to be on his back, limbs outstretched. He wasn't moving.

Someone groaned behind Longarm. He turned to see Suggs sitting gingerly on a rock, clutching the back of his left thigh with one hand. Blood showed on his forehead where he'd fallen on a rock. Raquella sat beside him, holding his arm and stretching her neck to see behind him.

"Where you hit?" Longarm said.

Suggs winced and lifted his head sharply as he clutched the back of his upper thigh. "None of your fucking business!"

Longarm grimaced. "I had a feelin'."

"I think the bullet went through without hittin' bone, but it's still gonna be a long ride back to Fort Sabre."

"Serves you right, waltzin' across the slope like a—"

A train whistle rose in the south. Longarm turned to see the train snaking up the tracks from two hundred yards away, chugging slowly up the gentle grade, too heavy with gold, no doubt, to move much faster than fifteen, twenty miles an hour.

Black coal smoke billowed from the locomotive's diamond-shaped stack, and steam wafted around the grinding iron wheels. Longarm sat on a boulder and watched the train move slowly into the arroyo, then begin to gain speed as the land flattened out.

"Yep," Suggs said behind him, his voice pinched with pain. "Movin' at that speed, they'd have been easy prey for those three Gatling guns. I just hope they don't stop. Might be a tad difficult, with all these dead *rurales* layin' about, to get our story across."

"They won't stop," Longarm said as the locomotive cleaved the arroyo between the ruined town and the ridge. "Not with all that gold on board. I just hope they don't get itchy trigger fingers and start shootin'."

Longarm leaned his rifle against the rock beside him and slid his gaze back past the locomotive and coal tender to the flat car where a half-dozen men in dark-blue uniforms sat, dangling their legs over the side of the car as they passed a couple of stout crock jugs back and forth between them.

A couple held rifles across their thighs and, spying Longarm, one of the men tensed, the celebratory smile fading from his lips. The others glanced at Longarm, and swept their bleary gazes across the slope covered with dead *rurales*.

One turned his head to yell behind him, and the three men crouched atop the express car raised their rifles and looked around cautiously. They continued swiveling their heads to watch the slope as the gold train continued north along the track, and then the last flat car, carrying more armed, drunk guards, passed between the slope and the church and continued chugging on up the track, retreating into the brassy distance until the train was little more than a thin shadow above the rails.

Longarm scowled and glanced at Suggs with disbelief. "Those boys were three sheets to the wind. If we hadn't taken out those Gatlings, they'd be where the *rurales* are."

"It is Christmas," said a girl's voice.

Longarm turned his head to look over his other shoulder. Rosa sat beside the padre on the low stone wall of the barricade. Three saddle horses stood nearby, grazing on the sparse, brown grass growing between boulders. Smiling, Rosa tipped her canteen over a bandanna and pressed the cloth over the wound high on the padre's right shoulder, which was exposed by the open robe and his peeled-down underwear shirt.

"It is?"

Suggs said, "Damn, I lost all track of time!"

"That is why they were celebrating," Raquella said, rising from the rock beside Suggs. "Let us go into the village and tend Señor Suggs and the padre, and have a celebration ourselves."

"Mine is just a scrape," said the padre. "I will hold up no Christmas celebration. But we must bury the dead . . . even such evil dead as they are."

Longarm shouldered his rifle, kicked over one of the dead *rurales*, and pulled a cigar from the man's tunic pocket. Lighting the cigar and puffing smoke, he regarded Baretto. "You were plumb crazy to follow that girl here, Padre. Might've gotten yourself killed."

"The *rurales* have been a blight on this province for many months now." The padre stood as Rosa draped his left arm around her neck and began leading him down the slope. "Sometimes, even a man of God must take action when the opportunity arises." He laughed as he and Rosa moved past Longarm. "Even if it is only to get shot!"

When Suggs hobbled off down the slope, using his rifle for a crutch, Raquella retrieved the horses and moved over to where Longarm sat, smoking and glancing around at the dead men slouched amongst the rocks.

He thought about St. George lying dead near the other Gatling gun. The man must have gone mad at Fort Sabre, and conspired with Santangelo to get out, and out of west Texas, once and for all. No doubt his cut of the stolen gold would have taken him and his high-bred daughter a long way in Mexico.

But he hadn't gotten far after all. Was his daughter still

at the fort, celebrating Christmas alone, or was she some-where in Mexico, waiting for him and the gold?

"You will go back to Texas now?" Raquella's voice pulled Longarm back to the ridge. She plucked the cigar from his fingers and placed it between her lips, puffing smoke as she gazed up at him.

"Gotta get the Gatlings back. What're you gonna do?"

"I have decided to stay with Rosa and the padre. I have nothing else to do. Nowhere else to go. In the spring, I might do a little prospecting in the Sierra Madre."

"Alone?"

"I can take care of myself."

Longarm chuckled and took the cigar back. "Yeah, you can at that."

He and the girl started down the slope, Raquella leading the horses by their bridle reins. Longarm rested the barrel of his Winchester on his right shoulder and tucked the cigar in a corner of his mouth.

"Señor Suggs will not be able to ride for several days," Raquella said, slanting a sly glance at the lawman.

"What do you have in mind?"

"You know."

"Yep." Longarm wrapped his arm across her slender shoulders, and she reached across her chest to squeeze his hand. "That hot springs is gonna feel mighty good to-night."

Watch for

**LONGARM IN HELL'S
HALF ACRE**

the 348th novel in the exciting LONGARM
series from Jove

Coming in November!

GIANT-SIZED ADVENTURE FROM AVENGING ANGEL LONGARM.

BY TABOR EVANS

2006 GIANT EDITION

LONGARM AND THE OUTLAW EMPRESS
978-0-515-14235-8

2007 GIANT EDITION

LONGARM AND THE GOLDEN EAGLE SHOOT-OUT
987-0-515-14358-4

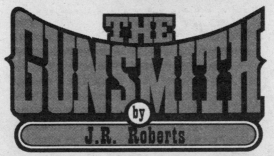

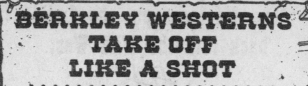